Georges Simenon

MADAME MAIGRET'S OWN CASE

A HELEN AND KURT WOLFF BOOK

HARCOURT BRACE JOVANOVICH, PUBLISHERS

San Diego   New York   London

The original French title was *L'Amie de Mme Maigret*, published in Paris, 1950. This English translation appeared, in somewhat different form, in the Crime Club series published by Doubleday & Company, Inc., 1959.

Library of Congress Cataloging-in-Publication Data
Simenon, Georges, 1903–1989.
    [Amie de Mme Maigret. English]
    Madame Maigret's own case / Georges Simenon.
      p.   cm.
    "A Helen and Kurt Wolff book."
    Translation of: L'amie de Mme Maigret.
    ISBN 0-15-154968-0
    I. Title.
  PQ2637.I53A773   1990
  843'.912—dc20   90-4274
Designed by Martha Roach
Printed in the United States of America
Second edition
A B C D E

MADAME MAIGRET'S OWN CASE

The "Nice Lady"
in Place d'Anvers

The chicken was on the stove, with a fine red carrot, a big onion, and a bunch of parsley with the stems sticking out. Madame Maigret bent over to make sure there was no risk that the gas, which she had turned down as low as possible, would go out. Then she closed the windows, except for the one in the bedroom, checked to be sure she hadn't forgotten anything, glanced in the mirror and, satisfied, left the apartment, locked the door, and put the key in her purse.

It was a little after ten o'clock on a March morning. The air was crisp, with sparkling sunshine over Paris. By walking as far as Place de la République she could have taken a bus going right to Boulevard Barbès and reached Place d'Anvers in plenty of time for her eleven o'clock appointment.

Because of the "nice lady," she went down the stairs to the Richard-Lenoir Métro station, just a step or two from her own door, and made the whole trip underground, at every stop looking vaguely at the familiar posters on the cream-colored walls.

Maigret had made fun of her, though not too much, since he had had a lot on his mind the last three weeks.

"Are you sure there isn't a good dentist nearer home?"

Madame Maigret had never before had any trouble with her teeth. Madame Roblin, their neighbor on the fourth floor—the one with the dog—had spoken so highly of Dr. Floresco that she had decided to go and see him.

"He has the fingers of a pianist. You won't even know he's working in your mouth. And because you've been recommended by me, he'll charge you only half the usual fee."

He was a Romanian who had his office on the fourth floor of a building on the corner of Rue Turgot and Avenue Trudaine, right opposite Place d'Anvers. Was this Madame Maigret's seventh or eighth visit? She had a regular appointment at eleven o'clock. It had become routine.

The first time, she had arrived a good quarter of an hour early, thanks to her morbid fear of keeping anyone waiting, and had twiddled her thumbs in a room overwarmed by a gas heater. On her second visit, she had also had to wait. Both times it was quarter past eleven before she was admitted to the dentist's office.

On the day of her third appointment, since there was bright sunshine and the square opposite was filled with the twittering of birds, she had decided to sit down on a bench and wait there. This was how she had made the acquaintance of the woman with the little boy.

By now the habit was so well established that she deliberately left early, and took the Métro in order to save time.

It was pleasant to see grass, and buds nearly bursting on the branches of the few trees outlined against the wall of the Collége Rollin. Sitting in full sunshine on the bench, she could follow the movements on Boulevard Rochechouart: the green-and-white buses, which looked like huge beasts, and the taxis darting in and out.

There was the woman, in a blue suit, just as on the other mornings, and her little white hat, which was so becoming to her and so springlike. She slid over to make more room for Madame Maigret, who had brought a chocolate bar with her and held it out to the child.

"Say thank you, dear."

He was two, and the most striking thing about him was his big black eyes and immensely long lashes, which made him look like a girl. At first, Madame Maigret had wondered whether he could talk, whether the syllables he uttered belonged to any language. Then she had realized, though she hadn't gone so far as to ask their nationality, that he and the woman were foreigners.

"To me, March is the most beautiful month in Paris, in spite of the showers," Madame Maigret said. "Some people prefer May or June, but March has so much more freshness."

She turned around from time to time to keep an eye on the dentist's windows. From where she was sitting, she could see the head of the patient who usually preceded her. He was a man of about fifty, rather unfriendly, who was in the process of having all his teeth out. She had become acquainted with him too. He had been born in Dunkerque, lived with his married daughter in this neighborhood, but didn't like his son-in-law.

3

The little boy, equipped this morning with a tiny red bucket and spade, was playing with the gravel. He was always very clean, very well cared for.

"I think I'll have to come only twice more." Madame Maigret sighed. "According to what Dr. Floresco told me, he's going to start on the last tooth today."

The woman smiled as she listened. She spoke excellent French, with a trace of accent that lent charm. Six or seven minutes before eleven, she was smiling at the child, who was greatly surprised at having thrown dust in his own face. Then all of a sudden she seemed to be looking at something on Avenue Trudaine, to be hesitating. She stood up and said urgently:

"Will you watch him for a minute? I'll be right back."

At the time, Madame Maigret didn't think too much about it. With her appointment in mind, she simply hoped the mother would be back in time, but she tactfully refrained from turning around to see where she was going.

The little boy hadn't noticed anything. He was still squatting there, filling his red bucket with pebbles, emptying it, and indomitably starting all over again.

Madame Maigret wasn't wearing a watch. Her watch hadn't run for years, and she never remembered to take it to the watchmaker. An old man came and sat down on the bench. He must have been a resident of the neighborhood, since she had seen him before.

"Would you be kind enough to tell me the time, monsieur?"

He must not have had a watch either, because he only answered:

"About eleven o'clock."

The head was no longer to be seen in the dentist's

window. Madame Maigret began to get anxious. She was ashamed to keep Dr. Floresco waiting; he was so nice, so gentle, and his patience was unfailing.

She looked all around the square without seeing the young woman in the white hat. Had she suddenly been taken ill? Or had she seen someone she wanted to speak to?

A policeman was walking through the square, and Madame Maigret stood up to ask him the time. It really was eleven o'clock.

The woman still did not come back, and the minutes were going by. The child had looked up at the bench and seen that his mother was no longer there, but he hadn't seemed to mind.

If only Madame Maigret could get in touch with the dentist! She would have to cross the street and go up three flights of stairs. She felt tempted to ask the old man to watch the little boy while she went up to explain to Dr. Floresco, but she didn't feel right about doing that. She remained standing, looking around with mounting impatience.

The second time she asked a passerby the time, it was twenty minutes past eleven. The old man had gone; she was alone now on the bench. She had seen the patient who preceded her come out of the corner building and walk off in the direction of Rue Rochechouart.

What should she do? Had something happened to the nice lady? If she had been knocked down by a car, there would have been a crowd, people running. Was the child going to get upset?

It was a ridiculous situation. Maigret would make fun of her again. It would be best not to mention it to him. She would telephone the dentist in a little while and apologize. Would she dare tell him what had happened?

Suddenly she felt hot, because her nervousness was making her blood tingle.

"What's your name?" she asked the child.

But he just looked at her out of his dark eyes without answering.

"Do you know where you live?"

He wasn't listening to her. It had already occurred to Madame Maigret that he might not understand French.

"Excuse me, monsieur. Could you tell me the time, please?"

"Twenty-two minutes to twelve, madame."

There was no sign of the mother. At noon, when neighborhood whistles blew and a nearby bar was invaded by bricklayers, she still hadn't returned.

Dr. Floresco came out of the building and got behind the wheel of a small black car. Yet she didn't dare leave the child to go and apologize.

What was on her mind now was her chicken, still on the stove. Maigret had told her that he would more than likely be home for lunch at about one.

Ought she to inform the police? But to do so she would have to leave the square. If she took the child with her and the mother came back in the meantime, the woman would be out of her mind with anxiety. Goodness knows where she would run off to then, or where they would finally catch up with each other! She couldn't leave a two-year-old baby alone in the middle of a square either, just a step or two from the buses and cars that passed in a steady stream.

"Excuse me, monsieur. Would you tell me what time it is?"

"Half past twelve."

The chicken was certainly beginning to burn; Maigret would be going in. It would be the first time in all these years of marriage that he hadn't found her at home.

It was impossible to telephone him too, because she would have to leave the square and go into a bar. If only she could see that policeman who had gone past earlier, or any policeman, she would tell him who she was and ask him to be kind enough to call her husband. As if it had been deliberately arranged, there wasn't one in sight. She looked in all directions; sat down; stood up again; kept thinking she saw the white hat; but it was never the one she was waiting for.

She counted more than twenty white hats in half an hour, and four of them were worn by women in blue suits.

At eleven o'clock, while Madame Maigret was beginning to be worried, detained in the middle of the square by responsibility for a child whose name she didn't even know, Maigret was putting on his hat, leaving his office, saying a few words to Inspector Lucas, and walking glumly toward the little door that connects the offices of the Police Judiciaire with the Palais de Justice.

It too had become a routine, dating from about the time Madame Maigret first went to her new dentist in the Ninth Arrondissement. The chief inspector entered the examining magistrates' corridor, where there were always some queer-looking birds waiting on the benches, some of them flanked by policemen, and knocked at the door that bore the name Dossin.

"Come in."

Dossin was the tallest magistrate in Paris and he always seemed to be embarrassed about it and to be apologizing

7

for having the aristocratic figure of a Russian wolfhound.

"Sit down, Maigret. Smoke your pipe if you want to. . . . Have you read this morning's story?"

"I haven't seen the papers yet."

The judge pushed one over to him with a big front-page headline:

STEUVELS CASE
ATTORNEY PHILIPPE LIOTARD
APPEALS TO HUMAN RIGHTS LEAGUE

"I've had a long talk with the public prosecutor," said Dossin. "He agrees with me. We can't release the book-binder. Even if we wanted to, Liotard would prevent us by his virulence."

A few weeks ago, this name had been all but unknown at the Palais. Philippe Liotard, who was not much over thirty, had never pleaded an important case. After having been an assistant to a famous lawyer for five years, he was just setting up his own practice. He still lived in an ordinary bachelor apartment on Rue Bergère, next door to a whorehouse.

Ever since the Steuvels case had broken, he had been mentioned in the papers every day. He gave sensational interviews, issued communiqués, and even appeared in newsreels, his forelock belligerent, his smile sarcastic.

"Nothing new with you?"

"Nothing worth reporting, Judge."

"Do you hope to find the man who sent the telegram?"

"Torrence is in Concarneau on that. He's a resourceful fellow."

In the three weeks it had held public attention in its

grip, the Steuvels case had run through a number of subheads, like a newspaper serial.

It had begun with:

THE CELLAR ON RUE DE TURENNE

By chance, the setting was a district Maigret knew well, one in which he even had a hankering to live, less than fifty yards from Place des Vosges.

Leaving narrow Rue des Francs-Bourgeois at the corner of the square and following Rue de Turenne toward Place de la République, one comes first, on the left, to a bistro painted yellow, then to a little restaurant called Crémerie Salmon. Right next door is a glass-fronted workshop with a low ceiling. On the dusty window are tarnished letters reading: *Fine Binding*. In the next shop, the widow Rancé runs an umbrella business.

Between these two is the main entrance, under an archway housing the concierge's lodge, and, on the other side of a courtyard, an old town house, now riddled with offices and apartments.

A BODY IN THE FURNACE?

What the public didn't know, because it had been carefully kept from the press, was that it was through sheer chance that the case had come to light. One morning, in the mailbox at the Police Judiciaire, a dirty piece of wrapping paper was found. On it was written: *The bookbinder on Rue de Turenne has burned a body in his furnace.*

It wasn't signed, of course. The note had wound up on Maigret's desk. Skeptical, he hadn't bothered one of

9

his veteran inspectors with it, but had sent Lapointe, a new and young man itching to distinguish himself.

Lapointe had discovered that there was indeed a book-binder on Rue de Turenne, a man from Flanders who had lived in France for more than twenty-five years. His name was Frans Steuvels. Posing as a sanitary inspector, Lapointe had gone through his premises, and returned with a detailed plan.

"Steuvels works in the shopwindow, so to speak, sir. The rear of the workshop, which gets darker as you get farther back from the street, is cut off by a wooden partition. Behind it the Steuvelses have fixed up their bedroom.

"A staircase leads to the basement, where there is a kitchen, plus a small room, where they have to keep the light on all day, which serves as a dining room, and also a cellar."

"With a furnace?"

"Yes. An old model, which doesn't seem to be in very good shape."

"Does it work?"

"It wasn't going this morning."

It was Lucas who had gone to Rue de Turenne at about five o'clock in the afternoon for an official search. Fortunately, he had taken a warrant with him, because the bookbinder had claimed "inviolability of domicile."

Lucas had nearly left empty-handed, and now that the case had turned into a nightmare for the Police Judi-ciaire, everyone was inclined to resent his partial success.

Sifting the ashes at the very back of the furnace, he had come upon two teeth, two human teeth. He had immediately taken them to the laboratory on his return.

"What kind of man is he, this bookbinder?" Maigret

10

had asked. At that point, he was only remotely connected with the case.

"He must be about forty-five. He's red-haired, pock-marked, has blue eyes and a gentle look. His wife, although she's younger than he is, never takes her eyes off him, as if he were a child."

They knew by now that Fernande, who had become notorious too, had come to Paris as a domestic servant and later had been on the streets for several years around Boulevard de Sébastopol.

She was thirty-six, had been living with Steuvels for ten years, and three years ago, for no apparent reason, they had been married in the town hall of the Third Arrondissement.

The laboratory had sent up its report. The teeth were those of a man of about thirty, probably fairly fat, who must have been alive a few days earlier.

Steuvels had been brought to Maigret's office, amicably, and the usual grilling had begun. He had sat in the green plush armchair facing the window, which overlooked the Seine. That evening it was pouring, and throughout the ten or twelve hours the interrogation had lasted, they had heard the rain beating against the windowpanes and the gurgling of water in the gutter. The bookbinder wore glasses with thick lenses and steel rims. His abundant, rather long hair was shaggy, and his tie was crooked.

He was a cultured man, however, who had read a lot. He remained calm and deliberate, though his delicate, ruddy skin flushed easily.

"How do you explain the fact that human teeth have been found in your furnace?"

"I don't explain it."

"Have you lost any teeth recently? Or your wife?"

"Neither one of us. Mine are false."

He had taken his plate out of his mouth, then put it back with a practiced movement.

"Can you give me an account of how you spent the evenings of February 16, 17, and 18?"

The interrogation had taken place on the evening of the twenty-first, after Lapointe and Lucas had been to Rue de Turenne.

"Do those dates include a Friday?"

"The sixteenth."

"In that case, I went to the Saint-Paul cinema on Rue Saint-Antoine, as I do every Friday."

"With your wife?"

"Yes."

"And the other two days?"

"Saturday afternoon, Fernande left."

"Where did she go?"

"To Concarneau."

"Had the trip been planned long before?"

"Her mother, who's a cripple, lives with her other daughter and her son-in-law in Concarneau. On Saturday morning, we received a telegram from her sister saying that their mother was seriously ill. So Fernande took the first train."

"Without telephoning?"

"They have no telephone."

"Was the mother very bad?"

"She wasn't ill at all. The telegram didn't come from Fernande's sister."

"Who did it come from then?"

"We don't know."

"Have tricks like this ever been played on you before?"

"No. Never."

"When did your wife get back?"

"On Tuesday. She took advantage of being there to spend a couple of days with her family."

"What did you do all that time?"

"I worked."

"One of the tenants of your building states that dense smoke was coming out of your chimney on Sunday."

"That's possible. It was cold."

This was true. That Sunday and Monday had been very cold days, and severe frost had been predicted for the suburbs.

"What suit were you wearing on Saturday evening?"

"The same one I'm wearing today."

"Did anyone come to see you after you closed?"

"Nobody except a client who called for a book. Do you want his name and address?"

It was a well-known man, a member of the Hundred Bibliophiles. Thanks to Liotard, more was to be heard of these men, who were nearly all important personalities.

"Your concierge, Madame Salazar, heard someone knock at your door that evening about nine o'clock. She says several people were talking excitedly."

"People talking on the sidewalk perhaps, but not in my place. It's entirely possible, if they were excited, as Madame Salazar claims, that they knocked against the window."

"How many suits do you own?"

"Since I have only one body and one head, I own only one suit and one hat, apart from the old trousers and sweater I wear for work."

He had been shown a navy-blue suit found in the wardrobe in his bedroom.

"What about this one?"

"That doesn't belong to me."

"How does it happen, then, to have been found in your room?"

"I've never seen it. Anybody might have put it there in my absence. I've been here six hours already."

"Do you mind slipping on the coat?"

It fit him.

"Do you see these stains that look like rust? They're blood, human blood, according to our experts. Futile attempts were made to get rid of them."

"I don't recognize this clothing."

"Madame Rancé, the umbrella woman, states that she often saw you wearing blue, especially on Fridays, when you were going to the movies."

"I did have another suit, and it was blue, but I got rid of it more than two months ago."

After this first interrogation, Maigret was gloomy. He had had a long conversation with Judge Dossin, after which both of them had gone to see the public prosecutor.

It was the latter who had assumed responsibility for the arrest.

"The experts are in agreement, aren't they? The rest, Maigret, is up to you. Go ahead. We cannot release that man."

By the next day, Liotard had emerged from the shadows, and, ever since, Maigret had had him at his heels like a snapping mongrel.

Among the newspaper subheads, there was one that had been quite successful:

THE PHANTOM SUITCASE

Young Lapointe had declared that when he looked around the premises as an alleged sanitary inspector, he

14

saw a reddish-brown suitcase sticking out from under a table in the workshop.

"It was an ordinary cheap suitcase, and I stumbled on it. I was surprised it hurt so much, and I realized why when I tried to lift it. It was very heavy."

Yet at five in the afternoon, when Lucas searched the place, the suitcase was no longer there. To be more precise, there was still a suitcase, also brown and also cheap, but Lapointe maintained that it was not the same one.

"That's the suitcase I took to Concarneau," Fernande had said. "We've never owned another one. We hardly travel at all."

Lapointe was unshakable; he swore it was not the same suitcase, that the first one was more reddish brown, and had its handle tied together with string.

"If I had had a suitcase to mend," Steuvels retorted, "I wouldn't have used string. Don't forget that I'm a bookbinder and a skilled leather worker."

Then Philippe Liotard had started collecting testimonials from bibliophiles, and it had turned out that Steuvels was one of the best bookbinders in Paris, possibly *the* best, and that collectors entrusted their delicate work to him, especially the restoration of antique bindings.

Everybody agreed that he was an even-tempered man, who spent almost all his time in his workshop. The police, it was said, were raking through his past, searching for the slightest equivocal detail, to no avail.

True, there was Fernande. Steuvels had known her when she was on the streets, and it was he who had taken her away from that. But there was absolutely nothing against Fernande either since that period back in the past.

Torrence had been in Concarneau for four days. At the post office the original of the telegram had been found; it was printed by hand in block letters. The postmistress thought she remembered that it was a woman who had handed it across the counter. Torrence was still searching, compiling a list of recent arrivals from Paris, questioning two hundred people a day.

"We are fed up with the so-called infallibility of Chief Inspector Maigret!" Maître Liotard had declared to a reporter.

And he made reference to some trouble in a local election in the Third Arrondissement, which might well have induced certain people to precipitate a scandal in the district for political ends.

Judge Dossin, too, was a target in the press, and these attacks, not always subtle, made him blush.

"You haven't a single new clue?" he asked Maigret.

"I'm still looking. There are ten of us looking—sometimes more—and we're interrogating some people for the twentieth time. Lucas is hoping to find the tailor who made the blue suit."

As always happens when a case arouses public attention, the police were receiving hundreds of letters a day, almost all of which sent them off on false trails, causing them to waste a great deal of time. Nevertheless, everything was scrupulously checked; even lunatics who claimed to know something were given a hearing.

At ten minutes to one, Maigret got out of the bus on the corner of Boulevard Voltaire and, glancing up at his windows, as he always did, was a little surprised to see that the one in the dining room was closed, in spite of the bright sun shining directly on it.

He walked heavily upstairs and turned the doorknob. The door didn't open. Occasionally, when Madame Maigret was dressing or undressing, she would lock the door. He opened it with his key and found himself in a cloud of blue smoke. He dashed into the kitchen to turn off the gas. In the casserole, all that was left of the chicken, carrot, and onion was a scorched crust.

He opened all the windows. When a panting Madame Maigret pushed open the door half an hour later, she found him sitting there with a hunk of bread and a piece of cheese.

"What time is it?"

"Half past one," he said calmly.

He had never seen her in such a state: her hat was crooked, her lip quivered tremulously.

"Whatever you do, don't laugh," she said.

"I'm not laughing."

"Don't scold me either. I couldn't help it. And I'd like to have seen you in my position. . . . To think that you're reduced to eating a piece of cheese for lunch!"

"The dentist?"

"I haven't seen the dentist. Since quarter of eleven I've been in the middle of Place d'Anvers, and nowhere else."

"Were you ill?"

"Have I ever been taken ill in my life? . . . No, it was because of the baby. And when he began to cry and create a scene, there I was, looking like a kidnapper."

"What baby? A baby what?"

"I told you about the lady in blue and her child, but you never listen to me. . . . The one I met on the bench while I was waiting for the dentist. This morning, she suddenly got up and went off, after asking me to watch the child for a minute."

"And she didn't come back? What did you do with the child?"

17

"She finally did come back, just a quarter of an hour ago. I came home in a taxi."

"What did she say when she came back?"

"To crown it all, she didn't explain. . . . I was in the middle of the square, stuck there like a scarecrow, with the little boy yelling fit to draw a crowd.

"I saw a taxi stopping on the corner of Avenue Trudaine and I recognized her white hat. She didn't bother to get out. She opened the door and beckoned. The child was running ahead of me, and I was afraid he'd get hit by a car. He reached the taxi first, and the door was closing by the time I got there.

" 'Tomorrow,' she called. 'I'll explain tomorrow. Forgive me. . . .'

"She didn't thank me. The taxi was already moving off in the direction of Rochechouart, and it turned left toward Pigalle."

She stopped, out of breath, and took off her hat with such a brusque movement that she rumpled her hair.

"Are you laughing?"

"Of course not."

"You may as well admit that you want to. . . . All the same, she did leave her child with a stranger for more than two hours. She doesn't even know my name."

"And you? Do you know hers?"

"No."

"Do you know where she lives?"

"I don't know anything at all, except that I missed my appointment, my good chicken is ruined, and you're eating a piece of cheese off a corner of the table like a . . . like a . . ."

Then, not able to find the word, she began to cry as she walked toward the bedroom to change her dress.

The Worries
of the Great Turenne

Maigret had a manner all his own of climbing the two flights of stairs at the Quai des Orfèvres: his expression was indifferent at the foot of the staircase, where light from outside struck it almost full strength; then it grew more and more preoccupied as he penetrated the gray shadows of the old building, as though office worries thrust themselves more heavily upon him as he drew nearer to them. By the time he passed the receptionist, he was definitely the chief.

Recently, he had got into the habit, both morning and afternoon, before pushing open his own door, of stopping by his inspectors' office and, his hat and coat still on, going through to see the Great Turenne.

This was the latest joke at headquarters, and it was indicative of the stature the Steuvels case had attained.

Lucas, who had been forced to take charge of centralizing information, collating it, and keeping it up to date, had quickly been swamped. It was also his job to answer telephone calls, open mail concerning the case, and interview informants.

Unable to work in the duty office, where the inspectors were constantly coming and going, he had taken refuge in an adjoining room, on the door of which a facetious hand had written: *The Great Turenne.*

As soon as any inspector finished an assignment or anyone came back from a job, a colleague would ask him:

"Are you free?"

"Yes."

"Go in and see the Great Turenne. He's hiring!"

It was true. Lucas never had enough staff for all the checking he had to do, and there was probably nobody left in the division who hadn't been sent at least once to Rue de Turenne.

They all knew the intersection near the bookbinder's workshop, with the three cafés: first the bistro on the corner of Rue des Francs-Bourgeois, then the Grand Turenne opposite, and, a hundred feet away, on the corner of Place des Vosges, the Tabac des Vosges, which the reporters had adopted as their headquarters—because they were in on the case too.

The inspectors took their drinks at the Grand Turenne, from the windows of which you could see the workshop of the Flemish bookbinder. This was *their* headquarters, and Lucas's office had turned into a sort of local branch.

Amazingly, good old Lucas, chained down by his classification work, was almost the only one who hadn't set foot on the scene of action since his visit there the first day.

20

Nevertheless, it was he who knew that corner better than any of them. He knew that next to the Grand Turenne came a high-class wineshop, Les Caves de Bourgogne, and he was acquainted with its proprietors; he needed only to consult a card to find out what they had told every investigator.

No. They hadn't seen anything. But on Saturday evenings they left for the Chevreuse Valley, where they spent the weekend in a cabin they had built themselves.

After Les Caves de Bourgogne came the shop of a shoemaker named Bousquet.

He, on the other hand, talked too much; but he had the defect of not telling everybody the same thing. It depended on what time of day he was questioned, how many aperitifs and brandies he had had at one of the three cafés, no matter which.

Then came Frère's stationery business, partly wholesale. At the rear of the courtyard was a manufacturer of cardboard.

Above Frans Steuvels' workshop, on the second floor of the old town house, jewelry was mass-produced. This was the firm of Sass & Lapinsky, which employed about twenty girls and four or five men, the latter all with difficult names.

Everybody had been questioned, some of them four or five times, by various inspectors, not to mention numerous inquiries by reporters. Two pine tables in Lucas's office were covered with papers, plans, memos. He was the only man who could find his way around in the muddle.

Indefatigably, he continued bringing the notes up to date. Once more, in the afternoon, Maigret took up a position behind Lucas, not saying anything, merely pulling gently on his pipe.

A page headed "Motives" was black with notes that had been crossed out, one by one.

They had looked for a political angle. Not in the direction Liotard had indicated, because that wouldn't hold up. But Steuvels, who lived like a recluse, might have belonged to some subversive organization.

This hadn't led anywhere. The deeper they looked into his life, the more they realized that it was unexceptional. The books in his library, examined one by one, were books by good writers of the whole world, selected by an intelligent, unusually cultured man. Not only had he read and reread them, but he'd made notes in the margins.

Jealousy? Hardly. Fernande never went out without him, except to do her marketing in the neighborhood, and from where he sat he could almost keep an eye on her in all the shops she went to.

They had wondered if there might be a connection between the presumed murder and the proximity of Sass & Lapinsky. But nothing had been stolen from the jewelry manufacturers, and neither the owner nor the employees knew the bookbinder, except by sight behind his window.

There was nothing to the Belgian angle either. Steuvels had left there at the age of eighteen and had never been back. He wasn't interested in politics, and there was no indication that he might belong to a Flemish extremist movement.

They had thought of everything. Lucas was accepting the craziest suggestions as a matter of duty. He would open the door to the inspectors' office and call one of them at random.

They knew what that meant. A new check to be made on Rue de Turenne or somewhere else.

"I may have hold of something," he said to Maigret this time, pouncing on a sheet of paper among the scattered files. "I had a notice sent out to all taxi drivers. One's just left, a naturalized Russian. I'll get it checked."

This was the current word: "Check!"

"I wanted to find out whether a taxi had taken anybody to the bookbinder's after dark on Saturday, February 17. This driver, named Georges Peskine, was hailed by three people that Saturday, at about quarter past eight, near the Gare Saint-Lazare. They told him to take them to the corner of Turenne and Francs-Bourgeois. So it was after half past eight when he dropped them, which doesn't fit too badly with the concierge's testimony about the noise she heard. The driver doesn't know who his fares were. But, according to him, the one who seemed the most important of the three, the one who spoke to him, was a Levantine."

"What language were they speaking to each other?"

"French. One of the others, a big, fair, rather heavy man of around thirty, blessed with a strong Hungarian accent, seemed to be worried, uneasy. The third, a middle-aged Frenchman, not so well dressed as his companions, didn't seem quite up to them socially.

"When they got out of the taxi, the Levantine paid, and all three walked back up Turenne toward the bookbinder's."

If it hadn't been for this business of the taxi, Maigret might never have thought of his wife's adventure.

"While you're working on taxi drivers, you might inquire about a little incident that happened this morning. It hasn't anything to do with the case, but it intrigues me."

Lucas wasn't prepared to be so sure that it had nothing to do with the case. By now he was ready to connect the

23

remotest, most fortuitous events with it. First thing every morning he had all the city police reports sent to him, to make sure they didn't contain anything that might be useful.

All alone in his office, he was coping with an enormous workload, of which the public, reading the papers and following the Steuvels case as though it were a serial, had not the least inkling.

Maigret briefly sketched the episode of the woman in the white hat and the little boy.

"You might also call our friends in the Ninth Arrondissement headquarters. The fact that she was on the same bench in Place d'Anvers every morning makes it seem likely that she lives in that neighborhood. Ask them to check that whole area, tradesmen, hotels, rooming houses."

Check, check! Normally, there were sometimes ten inspectors smoking, preparing reports, reading newspapers, or even playing cards in the next office. Now, almost never were there two at once.

Scarcely had they come in when the Great Turenne would open the door of his den. "Are you free, son? Come in here a minute."

And one or more of them would set off on a trail.

The missing suitcase had been hunted in the baggage rooms of all the stations and in all the pawnshops.

Lapointe may have been inexperienced, but he was a responsible young man, incapable of making up a story for his boss.

On the morning of February 21, therefore, there must have been in Steuvels' workshop a suitcase that was no longer there when Lucas appeared at five o'clock.

Yet, as far as the neighbors could recollect, Steuvels

had not left home that day, and no one had seen Fernande go out with a suitcase or package.

Had anyone stopped in to pick up finished binding work? This had also been "checked." The Argentine Embassy had sent for a document that Steuvels had created a sumptuous binding for, but it was not bulky, and the messenger had it under his arm when he left.

Martin, the most knowledgeable man at the PJ in this field, had worked for almost a week in the bookbinder's shop, examining his books, studying the work he was doing and had done during the last few months, getting in touch with his clients by telephone.

"He's an amazing man," was his conclusion. "He has the most select clientele you can imagine. They all have complete confidence in him. What's more, he works for several embassies."

This angle yielded nothing mysterious either. If the embassies entrusted their work to him, it was because he was a specialist in heraldry and owned the stamps for a large number of coats of arms, which enabled him to produce books or documents emblazoned with the arms of various countries.

"You don't look happy, Chief. But you'll see. Something will come out of all this in the end."

And good old Lucas, who never lost heart, pointed to the hundreds of pieces of paper he was blithely accumulating.

"We found some teeth in the furnace, didn't we? They didn't get there all by themselves. And someone sent a telegram from Concarneau to lure Steuvels' wife there. The blue suit hanging in the wardrobe had human bloodstains on it, which someone tried unsuccessfully to remove. . . . Liotard can carry on until he's blue in the face; he won't budge me on that."

25

But all this paperwork, so intoxicating to the inspector, overwhelmed his chief, who was looking at it with a jaundiced eye.

"What are you thinking, Chief?"

"Nothing. I'm just wondering."

"About releasing him?"

"No. That's the examining magistrate's business."

"Otherwise, you'd have him released, wouldn't you?"

"I don't know. I'm wondering whether to start the whole case over again from the beginning."

"Just as you like," replied Lucas, slightly offended.

"That doesn't prevent you from going ahead with your work. On the contrary. If we wait too long, we'll never get it straight. It's always the same: once the press in-terferes, everybody has something to say, and we're swamped."

"Still, I *have* found that taxi driver, and I'm going to find the one Madame Maigret saw too."

The chief inspector filled a fresh pipe and opened the door. There wasn't a single inspector next door. They had all gone off somewhere, busy about the man from Flanders.

"Have you made up your mind?" Lucas asked.

"I think so."

He didn't go to his own office, but left the PJ and immediately hailed a taxi.

"Corner of Turenne and Francs-Bourgeois."

Those words, heard from morning to night, were be-coming irritating.

The residents of the neighborhood, for their part, had never had such a time. All of them, one after the other, had had their names in the papers. All the shopkeepers

26

and workmen had to do was stop in the Grand Turenne for a drink and they met the inspectors; if they went across the street to the Tabac des Vosges, which was famous for its white wine, they were greeted by reporters.

Ten times, twenty times, they had been asked their opinion of Steuvels, of Fernande, and for details about their movements.

Since there wasn't even a body, when all was said and done—nothing but two teeth—the whole thing was not at all tragic; it seemed more like a game.

Maigret left the taxi opposite the Grand Turenne, glanced inside, saw none of his men, walked a few steps, and found himself in front of the bookbinder's workshop, where the window had been empty for the last three weeks. There was no bell; so he knocked, knowing that Fernande ought to be at home.

It was in the morning that she went out. Every day since the arrest of Frans, in fact, she had left at ten o'clock, carrying three small casseroles, which fit, one above another, in a frame with a handle. They were her husband's meals, which she carried to Santé prison by Métro.

Maigret knocked a second time, and saw her emerge from the stairway that connected the workshop with the basement. She recognized him, turned to speak to someone out of sight, and finally came to let him in.

She was in slippers and had on a checked apron. Seeing her like this, a little overweight, her face bare of makeup, no one would have recognized the woman who once walked the little streets around Boulevard de Sébastopol. She looked for all the world like a homebody, a meticulous housewife. And in normal times she was probably a cheerful soul.

"Is it me you want to see?" she asked, not without a suggestion of weariness.

"Is anyone with you?"

She did not answer. Maigret walked over to the stairs, went down a few steps, leaned over, and frowned.

He had already been informed of the presence in the neighborhood of Alfonsi, who liked to drink an aperitif with the reporters in the Tabac des Vosges but avoided setting foot in the Grand Turenne.

He was standing, very much at home, in the kitchen, where something was simmering on the stove. Though he was slightly embarrassed, he managed an ironic smile for the chief inspector.

"What are you doing here?"

"You can see for yourself. Visiting. Just like you. I have a right to, don't I?"

Alfonsi had once been attached to the Police Judiciaire, but not in Maigret's division. For a few years he had been in the Vice Squad, until it had finally been made clear to him that, in spite of his political pull, he was unwanted.

He was short and wore raised heels to make himself taller, possibly with a deck of cards inside his shoes, as some people hinted. He was always dressed with exaggerated elegance and had a big diamond, genuine or fake, on his finger.

He had opened a private detective agency on Rue Notre-Dame-de-Lorette, of which he was both proprietor and sole employee, assisted sometimes by a vague sort of secretary, who was primarily his mistress and with whom he was to be seen in the evenings in nightclubs.

When Maigret had been told of his presence on Rue de Turenne, the chief inspector had at first thought that the former policeman was trying to pick up bits of information that he could later sell to reporters.

Then he had discovered that he was in the pay of Philippe Liotard.

This was the first time Maigret had crossed Alfonsi's path in person, and he muttered:

"I'm waiting."

"What for?"

"For you to go."

"That's too bad, because I'm not through."

"Suit yourself."

Maigret made as though to leave.

"What are you going to do?"

"Have one of my men follow you day and night. I have a right to."

"That's fine with me. No need to get nasty, Monsieur Maigret."

He set off up the stairs with his air of being quite at home in the underworld, winking at Fernande before he left.

"Does he come here often?" asked Maigret.

"This is the second time."

"I advise you not to trust him."

"I know. I know that type."

Was this a discreet allusion to the days when she was at the mercy of the men in the Vice Squad?

"How is Steuvels?"

"All right. He reads all day long. He's confident."

"And you?"

Was there a hesitation?

"So am I."

Nonetheless, she was obviously wary.

"What books are you taking him now?"

"He's in the middle of rereading Marcel Proust all the way through."

"Have you read him too?"

"Yes."

Steuvels had, in fact, educated the wife he had picked up long ago in the gutter.

"You mustn't think I've come to see you as an enemy. You know the situation as well as I do. I want to understand. At the present time, I don't understand. Do you?"

"I'm sure Frans hasn't committed any crime."

"Do you love him?"

"That word doesn't mean anything. I'd need another word, a special one that doesn't exist."

He went up to the workshop again, where the bookbinder's tools were laid out on the long table facing the window. The presses were at the back, in semidarkness, and on the shelves books waiting their turn among the work in progress.

"He had regular habits, didn't he? I'd like you to tell me as accurately as possible how he spent his day."

"Somebody else asked me that already."

"Who?"

"Maître Liotard."

"Has it occurred to you that Maître Liotard's interests don't necessarily coincide with your own? He was unknown three weeks ago, and what he is after is to get as much publicity for himself as possible. It doesn't matter to him whether your husband is innocent or guilty."

"Excuse me, but if he proves his innocence, that will be a terrific boost for him, and his reputation will be made."

"And if he obtains your husband's release without having definitely proved his innocence? He'll make a name as a smart operator. He'll be in great demand. They'll say of your husband: 'Lucky for him Liotard got him off!' In other words, the guiltier Steuvels appears, the more credit Liotard will get. Do you realize that?"

"Frans realizes it, anyhow."

"Did he say so?"

"Yes."

"Doesn't he like Liotard? Why did he choose him?"

"He didn't choose him. Liotard himself—"

"Just a minute. You've said something important."

"I know."

"Did you do it on purpose?"

"Maybe I did. I'm sick of all this fuss around us, and I know where it's coming from. It doesn't seem to me that I'm doing Frans any harm by saying what I'm saying."

"When Inspector Lucas came to make his search on February 21 at about five o'clock, he didn't leave alone. He took your husband along with him."

"And you questioned him all night," she said reproachfully.

"That's my duty. . . . At that time, Steuvels had no lawyer, because he didn't know he was going to be held. Since then, he hasn't been released. He came back here for only a very short time, accompanied by the police. Yet when I told him to choose a lawyer, he named Liotard without any hesitation."

"I see what you mean."

"So the lawyer talked to Steuvels here *before* Lucas came?"

"Yes."

"Therefore it must have been on the afternoon of the twenty-first, between the visits of Inspectors Lapointe and Lucas."

"Yes."

"Were you present at the interview?"

"I was downstairs doing a thorough cleaning, because I'd been away three days."

"You don't know what they said to each other? They hadn't met before?"

"No."

"It wasn't your husband who telephoned to ask him to come?"

"I'm almost sure it wasn't."

Some neighborhood children had their faces pressed against the window, and Maigret asked:

"Would you rather we went downstairs?"

She led him through the kitchen to the little window-less room, which was very attractive, very cozy, with shelves of books all around, the table at which the couple had their meals, and, in a corner, another table, which served as a desk.

"You asked me how my husband spent his time. . . . He got up every day at six, winter and summer, and in winter the first thing he did was stoke the furnace."

"Why wasn't it going on the twenty-first?"

"It wasn't cold enough. After a few freezing days, remember, the weather turned mild again. . . . And neither of us feels the cold much. In the kitchen, I have the gas stove, which gives out enough heat, and there's another one in the workshop that Frans uses for his glue and his tools. . . .

"Before shaving he would go around to the bakery for croissants while I made the coffee, and we'd have breakfast.

"Then he would wash up and get to work. . . . I would leave about nine—after finishing most of my house-work—to do the marketing."

"He never went out to deliver work?"

"Hardly ever. People brought their work to him and called for it. When he had to go out, I used to go with him, because those were just about our only outings. . . .

"We had lunch at half past twelve."

"Would he go back to work right away?"

"Nearly always—after spending a few minutes in the doorway smoking a cigarette. He didn't smoke while he was working. . . .

"He worked until seven o'clock, sometimes half past seven. . . . I never knew what time we'd have dinner, because he always wanted to finish what he was working on. He'd put up the shutters, wash his hands, and after dinner we would read in this room until ten or eleven. Except on Friday evenings, when we went to the Saint-Paul cinema."

"He didn't drink?"

"A glass of brandy every night after dinner. Just one little glass, which would last him an hour. He never took more than a sip at a time."

"And Sundays? Did you go to the country?"

"Never. He hated the country. . . . We'd relax all morning, without getting dressed. He went in for carpentry a little. He made these shelves himself and just about everything we have here. . . . In the afternoon we'd go for a walk in the Francs-Bourgeois neighborhood, or on the Ile Saint-Louis. And we often had dinner at a little restaurant near Pont-Neuf."

"Is he stingy?"

She blushed and answered less spontaneously, with a question, as women do when they are embarrassed:

"Why do you ask me that?"

"He's been working at this rate for more than twenty years, hasn't he?"

33

"He's worked all his life. . . . His mother was very poor. He had an unhappy childhood."

"Yet he's supposed to be the most expensive book-binder in Paris, and he turns away more orders than he asks for."

"That's true."

"On what he makes, you could live comfortably, with a modern apartment and even a car."

"What for?"

"He maintains that he's never had more than one suit at a time, and your wardrobe doesn't seem any more extensive."

"I don't need anything. We eat well."

"You can't spend more than a third of what he earns for living expenses."

"I don't pay any attention to money matters."

"Most men work for some special goal. Some want a house in the country; others have dreams of retiring; others do it for the sake of their children. He has no children, has he?"

"Unfortunately, I can't have any."

"Before your time?"

"No. . . . He never knew any women, in a manner of speaking. He made do with you know what. And that's how I met him."

"What does he do with his money?"

"I don't know. I suppose he invests it."

They had, in fact, discovered a bank account in Steuvels' name at the Rue Saint-Antoine branch of the Société Générale. Nearly every week the bookbinder would deposit small sums, which corresponded to the amounts received from clients.

"He worked for the pleasure of working. He comes from Flanders, and I'm beginning to know what that means. He was capable of spending hours on a binding just for the joy of producing something out of the ordinary."

It was odd: sometimes she spoke of him in the past tense, as if the walls of Santé had already cut him off from the world; sometimes in the present, as if he would be home any minute.

"Did he keep in touch with his family?"

"He never knew his father. He was brought up by an uncle, who placed him in a charity institution when he was very young—luckily for him, because that's where he learned his trade. They were badly treated, and he doesn't like to talk about it."

Maigret observed that there was no exit from the apartment except the front door. To reach the court-yard, it was necessary to go out to the street and through the archway, passing the concierge's apartment.

It was amazing, at the Quai des Orfèvres, to hear Lucas rattling off all the names, which Maigret could hardly keep straight: Madame Salazar, the concierge; Made-moiselle Béguin, the fifth-floor tenant; the shoemaker; the umbrella woman; the restaurant proprietor and his chef—the whole lot of them, whom he talked about as though he had always known them and whose idiosyn-crasies he could list.

"What are you preparing for him tomorrow?"

"Ragout of lamb. He likes to eat. . . . Just now you seemed to be asking me what his chief interest is apart from work. It's probably food. And although he's sitting down all day and never gets any fresh air or exercise, I've never seen a man with such an appetite."

"Before he met you, did he have any men friends?"

"I don't think so. He's never mentioned them."

"Did he live here then?"

35

"Yes. He kept house for himself. Except that once a week Madame Salazar would come and clean up properly. . . . It may be because we don't need her anymore that she's never liked me."

"Do the neighbors know?"

"What I used to do? No. At least, they didn't until Frans was arrested. It was the reporters who brought that up."

"Are they cutting you?"

"Some of them. But Frans was so well liked that they're more inclined to be sorry for us."

This was true on the whole. If a poll had been taken in the street, the "fors" would certainly have won.

But the residents of the neighborhood didn't want it to be over too soon, any more than the newspaper readers did. The deeper the mystery, and the more bitter the contest between the Police Judiciaire and Philippe Liotard, the more delighted people were.

"What did Alfonsi want?"

"He didn't have time to tell me. He'd just arrived when you came. . . . I don't like the way he comes in here as if it were a public place, with his hat on his head, saying *tu* to me and calling me by my first name. If Frans were here, he'd have put him out long ago."

"Is he jealous?"

"He doesn't like familiarity."

"Does he love you?"

"I think so."

"Why?"

"I don't know. Perhaps because I love him."

He didn't smile. He hadn't kept his hat on, as Alfonsi had. He wasn't being rough, and he wasn't wearing his cagey expression either.

There in the basement he really looked like a man who is honestly trying to understand.

"Obviously you're not going to say anything that may be used against him."

"Of course not. Anyhow, I have nothing of the sort to say."

"Yet it's equally obvious that a man was killed in this basement."

"The experts say so, and I'm not educated enough to contradict them. In any case, it wasn't Frans."

"It seems impossible that it could have happened without his knowing."

"I know what you're going to say, but I tell you again that he's innocent."

Maigret stood up, sighing. He was glad she hadn't offered him a drink, as so many people feel obliged to do in such circumstances.

"I'm trying to start at the beginning again," he admitted. "My intention in coming here was to go over the scene inch by inch."

"You're not going to do that! They've turned everything upside down so many times!"

"I haven't the heart. I may come back. I'll probably have some more questions to ask you."

"You know that I tell Frans everything on visiting day?"

"Yes. I understand."

He started up the narrow stairs, and she followed him into the workshop, now almost dark, and opened the door for him. Both of them simultaneously noticed Alfonsi waiting at the corner.

"Are you going to let him in?"

"I'm wondering. I'm sick and tired of it all."

"Would you like me to tell him to leave you alone?"

"For tonight, at least."

"Good night."

She said good night too, and he walked heavily toward the former Vice Squad inspector. When he reached the corner, two young reporters were watching from the window of the Tabac des Vosges.

"Clear off."

"Why?"

"Because she doesn't want you bothering her again tonight."

"Why are you so hard on me?"

"Because I don't like your face."

Turning his back on Alfonsi, he conformed to tradition by going into the Grand Turenne for a glass of beer.

The Shady Hotel
on Rue Lepic

The sun was shining brightly, but there was a nip in the
air that produced a cloud of vapor at lips and froze
fingertips. Even so, Maigret had decided to stand outside
on the platform of the bus, and he was alternately grunt-
ing and smiling in spite of himself as he read the morning paper.

He was early. It was barely eight-thirty by his watch
when he entered the inspectors' office, at the very moment Janvier, perched on a table, was trying to get down,
hiding the newspaper from which he had been reading
aloud.

There were five or six inspectors there, mostly the
young ones, waiting for Lucas to give them their day's
orders. They avoided looking at the chief inspector, but
some of them who cast a furtive glance at him could
hardly keep a straight face.

They had no way of knowing that the story had

amused him just as much as it had them, and that it was simply to please them, because they expected it, that he was wearing his grouchy expression.

A headline was spread across three columns on the front page:

MME MAIGRET'S MISADVENTURE

The adventure of the previous day in Place d'Anvers was recounted down to the last detail. The only thing lacking was a photograph of the chief's wife and the little boy left in her care in such cavalier fashion.

Maigret pushed open Lucas's door. He had read the story too and had good reason to take the matter more seriously.

"I hope you didn't think I was responsible for it? . . . I was thunderstruck this morning when I opened the paper. Honestly, I didn't talk to a single reporter. Right after our conversation yesterday, I called Lamballe, at Ninth Arrondissement headquarters, and I had to tell him the story, but without mentioning your wife's name, when I asked him to try to find the taxi. . . . By the way, he just phoned to say that by sheer chance he's already found the driver. He's sending him over. The man will be here in a few minutes."

"Was there anyone in here when you called Lamballe?"

"Probably. There's always somebody in here. And no doubt the door to the inspectors' office was open. But who? . . . It frightens me to think there might be a leak right here."

"I suspected it yesterday. There was a leak as far back as February 21, because when you went to Rue de Tu-

40

renne to search the bookbinder's premises, Philippe Liotard had already been notified."

"Who could it be?"

"I don't know. But it could only be somebody here."

"That's why the suitcase was gone by the time I got there."

"More than likely."

"In that case, why didn't they dispose of the blood-stained suit too?"

"Perhaps they didn't think of it. Or they thought we wouldn't find out what kind of stains they were. Perhaps they didn't have time."

"Do you want me to question the inspectors, Chief?"

"I'll take care of it."

Lucas had not finished going through the mail, which was stacked up on the long table he was using as a desk.

"Anything interesting?"

"I don't know yet. I'll have to check. There are several tips about the suitcase, of course. An anonymous letter states simply that it hasn't left Rue de Turenne and that we must be blind not to find it. Another claims that the root of the matter is in Concarneau. A five-page letter, closely written, reveals, with supporting arguments, that the government itself fabricated the whole business out of nothing at all in order to divert attention from the cost of living."

Maigret went into his own office, took off his hat and coat, then, despite the mildness of the weather, filled to the brim the only coal stove still in existence at the Quai des Orfèvres: the one he had had such a hard time keeping possession of when central heating was installed.

Opening the inspectors' door a crack, he called in Lapointe, who had just arrived.

"Sit down."

He closed the door again carefully, told the young man once more to sit down, and walked around him once or twice, glancing at him curiously.

"You're ambitious, aren't you?"

"Yes, Chief Inspector. I'd like to have a career like yours. . . . You might think me presumptuous, I suppose."

"Are your parents well off?"

"No. My father's a bank clerk in Meulan. He had a hard time raising us decently—my sisters and me."

"Are you in love?"

He did not blush or get embarrassed.

"No. Not yet. I still have time. I'm only twenty-four, and I don't want to get married before I'm settled."

"Do you live by yourself in a furnished room?"

"Fortunately not. My youngest sister, Germaine, is in Paris too. She works for a publisher on the Left Bank. We share a place. At night she has time to cook for us, and that's a saving."

"Does she have a boyfriend?"

"She's only eighteen."

"The first time you went to Rue de Turenne, did you come straight back here?"

Lapointe suddenly blushed, and hesitated a moment before replying.

"No," he finally admitted. "I was so proud and happy at having discovered something that I treated myself to a taxi and went to Rue du Bac to tell Germaine about it."

"That's all, my boy. Thank you."

Lapointe, uneasy and worried, was reluctant to leave.

"Why did you ask me that?"

"I'm the one who asks the questions here. Later on, maybe you'll get a chance to do some interrogating too.

Were you in Lucas's office yesterday when he telephoned the Ninth Arrondissement?"

"I was in the inspectors' office, and the door between was open."

"What time did you talk to your sister?"

"How do you know I did?"

"Answer me."

"She gets off work at five. She waited for me, as she often does, at the Big Clock Bar. We had a drink together before going home."

"Were you with her all evening?"

"She went to the movies with a girlfriend."

"Did you see her girlfriend?"

"No. But I know her."

"That's all. You can go," Maigret said.

He would have liked to offer an explanation, but someone came to tell him that a taxi driver was asking to see him.

This was a big, red-faced man of around fifty, who must have driven a hackney coach in his younger days and who, judging by his breath, had certainly swallowed several glasses of white wine for the good of his stomach before reporting.

"Inspector Lamballe told me to come and see you about the young lady."

"How did he find out it was you who picked her up?"

"I usually wait on Place Pigalle, and he came over for a word with me last night, the same way he had a word with all of us. . . . It was me who picked her up."

"What time? Where?"

"It must have been about one o'clock. I was finishing my lunch at a restaurant on Rue Lepic. My taxi was outside. . . . I saw a couple leaving the hotel opposite, and the woman immediately made a dash for my taxi.

43

She seemed to be disappointed when she saw the flag was down. Since I'd got as far as my liqueur, I stood up and called across the street to her to wait."

"What was her companion like?"

"A fat little man, well dressed. Looked like a foreigner . . . Between forty and fifty; I can't say exactly. I didn't look at him much. He was facing her and was talking in a foreign language."

"What language?"

"I don't know. I come from Pantin, and I've never been able to tell one lingo from another."

"What address did she give?"

"She was jumpy, impatient. She asked me to go through Place d'Anvers first and slow down. She looked out the window.

"Then she said: 'Stop a minute, and drive on again when I tell you.'

"She beckoned to somebody. A motherly old soul was walking toward us with a little boy. The lady opened the door, pulled the kid in, and ordered me to drive on."

"Didn't it look to you like a kidnapping?"

"No. Because she spoke to the other lady. Not for long. Just a few words . . . And the lady seemed more relieved than anything else."

"Where did you take the mother and child?"

"First to Porte de Neuilly. There, she changed her mind and asked me to drive to the Gare Saint-Lazare."

"Did she get out there?"

"No. She stopped me on Place Saint-Augustin. . . . I got caught in traffic there, and I saw her in my mirror hailing another taxi, one of the Urbaine's, but I didn't have time to get its number."

"Did you try to?"

"Out of habit. She was really upset. And it *was* queer, after taking me all the way to Porte de Neuilly, to stop me on Place Saint-Augustin just to get in another taxi."

"Did she talk to the child on the way?"

"A sentence or two, to keep him quiet. . . . Is there a reward?"

"There may be. I don't know yet."

"You see, I've wasted my morning."

Maigret handed him some money, and a few minutes later was pushing open the door of the director, where the daily briefing had begun. The division heads were grouped around the big mahogany desk, talking quietly about current cases.

"What about you, Maigret? And Steuvels?"

From their smiles, it was obvious they had all read the morning paper's story. Once more, and again just to please them, he pretended to be disgruntled.

It was half past nine. The telephone rang. The director answered and handed it to Maigret.

"Torrence wants to speak to you."

Torrence's voice at the other end of the line was excited.

"Is that you, Chief? You haven't found the woman in the white hat? . . . The Paris paper's just arrived, and I've read the story. Well, the description fits someone I'm on the track of here."

"Go on."

"Since there's no way of getting anything out of the fool of a postmistress here, who's pretending to have lost her memory, I started checking the hotels and rooming houses, and questioning garagemen and railway-station employees."

"I know."

"The season hasn't started yet, and most of the people arriving in Concarneau are local residents or people who are more or less familiar—salesmen and—"

"Make it short."

He was aware that all conversation around him had stopped.

"I was thinking that if someone had come from Paris or somewhere else in order to send the telegram—"

"Yes, yes. I know what you thought."

"Well! A young lady in a blue suit and a white hat arrived the very evening the telegram was sent. She came on the four o'clock train, and the message was handed in at quarter of five."

"Did she have any luggage?"

"No . . . Wait. She didn't stay at a hotel. Do you know the Yellow Dog Hotel down by the pier? She had dinner there and sat in a corner of the café until eleven o'clock. In other words, she left again on the eleven-forty train."

"Have you verified that?"

"I haven't had time yet, but I feel pretty sure because she left the café at exactly the right time and she'd asked for the timetable right after she'd had dinner."

"Didn't she speak to anyone?"

"Only to the waitress. She read the whole time, even while she was eating."

"Have you been able to find out what kind of book she was reading?"

"No. The waitress says she had a foreign accent, but she doesn't know what it was. . . . What shall I do?"

"Go back and see the postmistress, of course."

"And after that?"

"Call me—or Lucas, if I'm not in the office. Then come back."

"All right, Chief. Do you think it's the same person too?"

When he hung up, Maigret had a little spark in his eyes.

"Maybe Madame Maigret will be the one who puts us on the track," he said. "Will you excuse me, Chief? I have some urgent checking to do."

By chance, Lapointe was still in the inspectors' office, visibly worried.

"You there, come with me!"

They took one of the taxis lined up on the quay.

Lapointe didn't feel any less worried, even though it was the first time the chief inspector had taken him out with him like this.

"Corner of Place Blanche and Rue Lepic."

It was the time of day when, in Montmartre and especially on Rue Lepic, carts were lined up along the sidewalks piled high with vegetables and fruit fragrant with the smell of earth and springtime.

Maigret recognized on the left the little table d'hôte restaurant where the taxi driver had had lunch and, opposite, the Hotel Beauséjour. Its narrow doorway was visible between a delicatessen and a grocery.

ROOMS BY MONTH, WEEK, DAY.
RUNNING WATER. CENTRAL HEATING.
REASONABLE RATES.

There was a glass door down the hallway, then a staircase, with a sign on the wall: *Office*. A hand, drawn with black ink, pointed upstairs.

"Anyone there?" he called.

The smell reminded him of the time when, just about

47

Lapointe's age and in the Hotels Squad, he used to spend his days going from one rooming house to another. The smell was a mixture of dirty laundry and sweat, unmade beds, slop pails, and food being warmed up on spirit lamps.

A slatternly woman with red hair leaned over the banister.

"What is it?"

Suddenly realizing that it was the police, she snapped crossly:

"I'm coming."

She took her time upstairs, moving buckets and brooms. Finally she appeared, buttoning her blouse over her protruding bosom. At closer range, her hair proved to be almost white at the roots.

"What's the matter? They checked here only yesterday. And I have nothing but quiet tenants. . . . You're not from the "Flophouse Squad," are you?"

Without answering, he described to her, as far as the taxi driver's testimony permitted, the companion of the woman with the white hat.

"Do you know him?"

"I may. I'm not sure. What's his name?"

"That's what I'd like to know."

"Do you want to see my book?"

"First I want you to tell me whether you have a tenant who looks like him."

"Nobody but Monsieur Levine."

"Who's he?"

"I don't know. . . . A very decent man, anyhow, who paid for a week in advance."

"Is he still here?"

"No. He left yesterday."

"Alone?"

"With the little boy, of course."

"And the woman?"

"Do you mean the nursemaid?"

"Just a minute. Let's begin at the beginning—to save time."

"That'll be fine, because I don't have any to spare. What's Monsieur Levine done?"

"Just answer my questions, will you? When did he arrive?"

"Four days ago. You can check my book. I told him I didn't have a vacant room, and it was true. He insisted. So I asked him for how long, and he told me he'd pay for a week in advance."

"How could you accommodate him if you had no room?"

Maigret knew the answer, but he wanted to make her say it. In this kind of hotel, the third-floor rooms are generally reserved for transient couples who come in for a few minutes or an hour.

"There are always the rooms for the casual trade," she replied, using the traditional term.

"Was the child with him?"

"Not then. He went away and came back with him an hour later. I asked him how he was going to manage with such a young child, and he told me that a nursemaid he knew would take care of him most of the day."

"Did he show you his passport or his identity card?"

According to regulations, she should have asked for one of these documents, but she obviously hadn't.

"He filled out the slip himself. . . . I saw right away that he was a respectable man. . . . Are you going to make trouble for me just for that?"

"Not necessarily. How was the nursemaid dressed?"

"In a blue suit."

"With a white hat?"

"Yes. She came in the morning and gave the boy his bath. Then she'd take him out."

"And Monsieur Levine?"

"He hung around in his room until eleven or twelve. I think he went back to bed. Then he'd go out, and I didn't see him again all day."

"And the child?"

"Nor him either. Not much before seven. It was the nursemaid who brought him back and put him to bed. She lay down on the bed fully dressed while she waited for Monsieur Levine to come home."

"What time did he come in?"

"Not before one."

"Would she leave then?"

"Yes."

"You don't know where she lived?"

"No . . . I know she took a taxi when she left, because I saw her."

"Was she intimate with your tenant?"

"Do you mean did they sleep together? I'm not sure. From certain indications, I think they did sometimes. . . . They have a right to, haven't they?"

"What nationality did Monsieur Levine write down on the reservation slip?"

"French. He told me he'd been in France a long time and was naturalized."

"Where did he come from?"

"I don't remember. . . . A man from the Flophouse Squad picked up the slips yesterday; he does every Tuesday. . . . From Bordeaux, I think."

"What happened yesterday at noon?"

"I don't know anything about noon."

"During the morning then?"

"Someone came and asked for him about ten o'clock. The nursemaid and the boy had been gone quite a while."

"Who?"

"I didn't ask his name. An ordinary little man, not very well dressed, shabby even."

"French?"

"Yes. I told him the room number."

"He'd never been here before?"

"No one had ever come to see him but the nursemaid."

"Did he have a southern accent?"

"More like a Paris accent. You know, the kind a man has who stops you in the street and tries to sell you fancy postcards or take you Lord knows where."

"Did he stay long?"

"Well, he stayed up there while Monsieur Levine was checking out."

"With his luggage?"

"How did you know? I was amazed to see him bringing his luggage down."

"Did he have much?"

"Four suitcases."

"Brown ones?"

"Nearly all suitcases are brown, aren't they? Anyhow, these were good quality; at least two of them were real leather."

"What did he say to you?"

"That he had to go away unexpectedly; that he'd be leaving Paris, but he'd be back in a little while for the boy's things."

"How much later did he come back?"

"About an hour. The nursemaid was with him."

"Weren't you surprised not to see the little boy?"

"So you know that too?"

51

She was growing more cautious, beginning to suspect that the matter was of some importance and that the police knew more about it than Maigret wanted to tell her.

"All three of them stayed in the room quite a while. They were talking pretty loud."

"As if they were quarreling?"

"As if they were arguing at least."

"In French?"

"No."

"Did the Frenchman take part in the conversation?"

"Not much . . . Anyhow, he left first, and I didn't see him again. Then later, Monsieur Levine and the nurse-maid left. As they passed me, he thanked me and told me they expected to be back in a few days."

"Didn't it seem strange to you?"

"If you'd kept a hotel like this one for eighteen years, nothing would seem strange to you."

"Did you clean the room yourself afterward?"

"I helped the maid."

"Did you find anything?"

"Cigarette butts all over the place. He smoked more than fifty a day. American cigarettes. And newspapers. He bought almost all the Paris papers."

"No foreign newspapers?"

"No. I thought of that."

"So you were curious?"

"You always like to know what's going on."

"What else?"

"The usual—a broken comb, torn underwear, some of the boy's things . . ."

"Any initials?"

"No."

"Good quality?"

"Pretty good, yes. Better than I'm used to seeing around here."

"I'll be back to see you again."

"What for?"

"Because some details that escape you at present will certainly come back to you when you think it over. . . . You've always been on good terms with the police, haven't you? The Hotels Squad doesn't bother you too much, does it?"

"I understand. But I don't know anything else."

"Good morning."

He and Lapointe were back on the sunny sidewalk in the midst of the bustle.

"A little drink?" suggested the chief inspector.

"I don't drink."

"You're quite right. . . . Have you thought things over in the meantime?"

The young man knew that he wasn't talking about what they had found out at the hotel.

"Yes."

"Well?"

"I'll speak to her tonight."

"Do you know who it is?"

"I have a friend who's a reporter on the paper that printed that story this morning, but I didn't see him yesterday. Anyway, I never talk to him about what goes on at headquarters. He often teases me about that."

"Does your sister know him?"

"Yes. But I didn't think they were dating. If I tell our father, he'll make her go back to Meulan."

"What's the reporter's name?"

"Bizard. Antoine Bizard. He lives alone in Paris. His family is in Corrèze. He's two years younger than I am, but some of his stories carry his own byline already."

"Do you meet your sister at lunchtime?"

"It depends. When I'm free and not too far from Rue du Bac, I eat with her in a little restaurant near her office."

"Go and meet her today. Tell her what we found out this morning."

"You really want me to?"

"Yes."

"What if she passes this on too?"

"She will."

"Is that what you want her to do?"

"Go ahead. But be sure to be nice to her. Don't let it look as if you're suspicious of her."

"But I can't have her going out with a man, whatever happens. My father told me to be sure—"

"Go on."

Maigret walked down Rue Notre-Dame-de-Lorette, just for the pleasure of walking, and took a taxi only at Faubourg Montmartre, after stopping for a glass of beer.

"Quai des Orfèvres."

Then he changed his mind and rapped on the glass.

"No. Go down Rue de Turenne."

He saw that Steuvels' workshop had its door shut, as it did every morning now, because Fernande must be on her way to Santé with her stack of casseroles.

"Stop a minute."

Janvier was at the bar of the Grand Turenne and, seeing the chief, gave him a wink. What new item had Lucas told him to check? He was deep in conversation with the shoemaker and two plasterers in white overalls. The milky tint of their Pernods could be seen from quite a distance.

"Turn left. Drive through Place des Vosges and Rue de Birague."

54

This meant passing the Tabac des Vosges, where Alfonsi was sitting alone at a little table near the window.

"Stop again."

"Are you getting out?"

"Yes. Wait for me."

It was the Grand Turenne he entered, after all, to have a word with Janvier.

"Alfonsi's across the street. Have you seen any reporters over there this morning?"

"Two or three."

"Know them?"

"Not all of them."

"Do you have much more to do?"

"Nothing much. If you have something for me, I'm free. I just wanted to talk to the shoemaker."

They had moved away from the group and were speaking in low voices.

"Something occurred to me after I read the story in the paper," Janvier continued. "The old shoemaker talks far too much, you know. He's determined to be noticed, and he'll make things up if necessary. Besides, every time he has something to tell, it means a few drinks for him. . . . Seeing that he lives right opposite Steuvels' place and works in his window too, I asked him whether any women ever came to see the bookbinder."

"What did he say?"

"Not much. He remembers one old one in particular: she must be rich, he says, because she comes in a limousine, with a chauffeur in livery who carries her books. . . . Also, about a month ago, a very elegant young woman in a mink coat. . . . Wait! I made a point of finding out if she came only once. He says not. She came again a couple of weeks ago, in a blue suit and a white hat. It was a day when the weather was beautiful, and the paper carried an article on the chestnut tree on Boulevard Saint-Germain."

"We can trace that."

"That's what I thought."

"Did she go down to the basement?"

"No. But I'm suspicious. He'd read the article too—that's obvious—and it's entirely possible that he's making it all up, just to get some attention. . . . What do you want me to do?"

"Keep an eye on Alfonsi. Don't let him out of your sight all day. Make a list of the people he speaks to."

"He's not supposed to know I'm following him?"

"It doesn't matter much if he does."

"What if he speaks to me?"

"Answer him."

Maigret went out with the smell of Pernod in his nostrils, and his taxi dropped him at the PJ. There, he found Lucas in the middle of lunch, which consisted of sandwiches. There were two glasses of beer on the desk, and the chief inspector took one of them without compunction.

"Torrence just phoned. The postmistress thinks she remembers a customer with a white hat, but she can't swear she's the one who handed in that telegram. According to Torrence, even if she were dead sure, she wouldn't say so."

"Is he coming back?"

"He'll be in Paris tonight."

"Call the Urbaine Taxi Company, will you? There's another taxi to be traced, maybe two."

Had Madame Maigret, who had another appointment with her dentist, left early, as she had the previous times, in order to spend a few minutes on the bench in the Place d'Anvers park?

Maigret didn't go home to Boulevard Richard-Lenoir for lunch. Lucas's sandwiches had looked tempting, so he had some sent up from the Brasserie Dauphine for himself.

This was usually a good sign.

Fernande's Adventure

Lapointe, red-eyed and rumpled, like somebody who has slept on a bench in a third-class waiting room, gave Maigret a look of such distress when the latter entered the inspectors' office that the chief immediately took him into his own office.

"The whole Hotel Beauséjour story is in the paper," said the young man lugubriously.

"That's good! I'd have been disappointed if it hadn't been."

Then Maigret deliberately began to talk to him as he would have talked to one of the old hands, to Lucas or Torrence, for instance.

"There are some people we know almost nothing about, not even whether they've really played any part in this case. There's a woman, a little boy, a rather stout man, and a man who looks seedy. Are they still in Paris? We don't know. If they are, they've probably split up.

The woman has only to take off her white hat and get rid of the child and we won't recognize her anymore. Do you follow me?"

"Yes, Chief Inspector. I think I understand. . . . But all the same, I don't like to think that my sister saw that fellow again last night."

"You can worry about your sister later. Right now, you're working with me. This morning's newspaper story will have alarmed them. There are two possibilities: they'll stay holed up, if they have a spot to hole up, or they'll look for a safer hiding place. In either case, our only chance is for them to do something to give themselves away."

"Yes."

At that point, Judge Dossin telephoned to express his surprise at the paper's disclosures, and Maigret had to sum up the position again.

"Everybody's been alerted, Judge: stations, airports, cheap hotels, highway police. Moers, up in Criminal Records, is busy looking for pictures that might correspond to our customers. We're questioning taxi drivers and, in case they have a car, garagemen."

"Do you think this has some connection with the Steuvels case?"

"It's a lead—after so many that haven't got us anywhere."

"I'm having Steuvels brought up this morning at eleven. His lawyer will be here, as usual; he won't let me exchange two words with his client except in his presence."

"Would you permit me to come in for a minute during your interrogation?"

"Liotard will protest, but come anyway. It won't look as if we'd planned it."

It seemed curious, but Maigret had never met this Liotard, who had become, in the press, at all events, something like a personal enemy.

This morning, all the papers again carried the young lawyer's comments on the latest angles of the case.

Maigret is a policeman of the old school, of the period when the gentlemen of the Police Judiciaire could, if they chose, give a man the third degree until weariness drove him to admit everything, keep him in their hands for weeks, pry shamelessly into people's private lives—a period when any kind of trick was considered legitimate.

He is the only person who doesn't realize that, to an informed public, tricks like these constitute nothing but monkey business.

What is it all about, really?

He has let himself be fooled by an anonymous letter, the work of a prankster. He has had an honest man locked up and has been incapable ever since of pinning any serious charge on him.

He won't give up. Rather than admit defeat, he is trying to gain time by playing to the gallery, calling Madame Maigret to the rescue, serving up to the public slices of cheap fiction.

Believe me, gentlemen, Maigret is out of date.

"Stay here with me, my boy," the chief inspector said to young Lapointe. "Only, tonight, before you go home, ask me what you may tell your sister, won't you?"

"I'll never tell her anything again."

"You tell her what I ask you to tell her."

From then on, Lapointe acted as his aide-de-camp. And that really meant something, for the Police Judiciaire was becoming more and more like a military headquarters.

The office of Lucas, the Great Turenne, represented the command post, to which runners made their way from all floors. Downstairs, several men of the Hotels Squad were busy going through registrations in search of a Levine or anybody else who might possibly be connected with the trio and the child.

The previous night, in most cheap hotels the guests had had the unpleasant surprise of being awakened by the police, who had examined their documents. This had resulted in some fifty men and women whose papers were not in order spending the rest of the night in the lockup at headquarters, where they were now lined up outside the Criminal Records Office.

In railway stations, travelers were being scrutinized without knowing it. Two hours after the papers came out, telephone calls began, and soon were so numerous that Lucas had to detail an inspector to this one job.

People had seen the little boy all over the place, in the most widely separated parts of Paris and the suburbs. Some had seen him with the woman in the white hat; some, with the gentleman with the foreign accent.

Pedestrians would suddenly rush up to a policeman and say:

"Hurry! The child's at the corner."

Everything was checked; everything *had* to be checked, if no chance was to be overlooked. Three inspectors had gone out first thing to interrogate garagemen.

And all night long the men of the Morals Squad had been on the job too. Hadn't the proprietress of the Beauséjour said that her tenant hardly ever came home before one o'clock?

Their task was to find out if he was a regular patron of nightclubs, to question bartenders and bar girls.

Maigret, after sitting through the daily briefing in the

director's office, prowled through the building, with Lapointe at his side most of the time—going down to the
Hotels Squad and up to Moers in Criminal Records,
taking a telephone call here, a statement there.

It was just after ten o'clock when a driver from the
Urbaine Company phoned. He hadn't called earlier because he had made a trip out of town, to Dreux, with
an old invalid who did not want to go by train.

It was he who had picked up the young woman and
the little boy on Place Saint-Augustin; he remembered
it perfectly well.

"Where did you take them?"

"The corner of Rue Montmartre and the Grands
Boulevards."

"Was there anyone waiting for them?"

"I didn't notice anyone."

"You don't know which way they went?"

"I lost sight of them right away in the crowd."

There were several hotels in the vicinity.

"Call the Hotels Squad again," Maigret said to Lapointe. "Tell them to go over that area again with a fine-
tooth comb. Do you realize now that, if they don't lose
their heads, if they don't budge, we haven't the remotest
chance of finding them?"

Torrence, back from Concarneau, had gone for a stroll
down Rue de Turenne, to get back into the feel of it,
he said.

As for Janvier, he had sent in a report on his shad-
owing assignment and was still on Alfonsi's tail.

The latter had joined Philippe Liotard the night before in a restaurant on Rue de Richelieu, where they
had had a good dinner and chatted quietly. Two women
had joined them later, neither of whom bore any resemblance to the young woman in the white hat. One was

the lawyer's secretary, a big blonde with the look of a movie starlet. The other had left with Alfonsi.

They had gone to the movies, near the Opéra, then to a nightclub on Rue Blanche, where they had stayed until two o'clock in the morning.

After that the private detective had taken his companion to the hotel where he lived, on Rue de Douai.

Janvier had taken a room at the same hotel. He had just phoned:

"They're not up yet. I'm waiting."

A little before eleven, Lapointe, following Maigret, was introduced to a part of the Quai des Orfèvres that was unknown to him. On the ground floor, they went down a long deserted corridor, the windows of which overlooked the courtyard. Reaching a corner, Maigret made a sign to the young man to keep quiet.

A police van passed through the entrance gates to headquarters, and entered the courtyard. Three or four policemen, smoking cigarettes, were waiting. Two others got out of the Black Maria, from which they unloaded a great brute of a man with a low forehead and handcuffs on his wrists. Maigret didn't know him; this one hadn't crossed his path.

Next came a fragile-looking old woman who might have been the chair custodian in a church, but whom he had arrested at least twenty times as a pickpocket. She followed her policeman like an old-timer, trotting along behind him with little steps in her extra-wide skirts, and would make the right turns for the examining magistrates' offices without being told.

The sun was bright, the air steely blue in the patches of shade, with whiffs of springtime, and there were a few newly hatched flies buzzing.

Frans Steuvels' red head appeared, bare of hat or cap;

his suit was quite crushed. He stopped, as though surprised by the sun, and his eyes were undoubtedly half closing behind his thick glasses.

He had been handcuffed, just like the brute. It was a regulation strictly enforced since several prisoners had escaped from this very courtyard, the latest of them via the corridors of the Palais de Justice.

With his hunched back and his flabby figure, Steuvels was typical of those intellectual craftsmen who read everything that comes their way and have no consuming interest outside their work.

One of the guards handed him a lighted cigarette. He thanked him and took a few drags on it with satisfaction, filling his lungs with air and tobacco.

He must have been easy to handle, because they were treating him kindly; they gave him time to stretch his legs before taking him over to the door. He seemed not to bear his guards any ill will and showed no rancor, no emotion.

There was a tiny bit of truth in Liotard's latest statement. Normally, Maigret himself would have completed the inquiry before turning the man over to the examining magistrate.

If it had not been for the lawyer, who had appeared on the scene as soon as the first interrogation was over, Maigret would have seen Steuvels several more times, which would have given him a chance to study him.

Instead, he scarcely knew him, having been alone with the bookbinder for only ten or twelve hours, at a time when he still knew nothing about him or about the case.

Rarely had he been confronted with a prisoner so calm, so much in control of himself, and there had been no indication that this was an assumed attitude.

Steuvels had waited for the questions, head down, with

an air of trying to understand, and he had watched Maigret as he would have watched a lecturer developing complicated ideas.

He had taken time to think, and then had answered in a gentle, rather faint voice, in carefully chosen phrases, which, however, held no affectation.

He had not become impatient, as most prisoners do, and when the same question had come up for the twentieth time, he had answered in the same terms, with remarkable equanimity.

Maigret would have liked to know him better, but for the last three weeks the man hadn't belonged to him, but to Dossin, who had him brought in, with his lawyer, about twice a week.

Fundamentally, Steuvels must be a shy man. And strangely, the examining magistrate was a shy man too. Noticing the initial G. before his name, the chief inspector had once made so bold as to ask him what it stood for, and the distinguished man had blushed.

"Don't tell anyone, or they'll start calling me Angel again, as my fellow students did at school, and later in law school too. My first name is Gabriel!"

"Now," Maigret said to Lapointe. "I want you to go and sit in my office, and take all messages until I come."

He did not go upstairs right away. He wandered through the corridors for a while, his pipe between his teeth, his hands in his pockets, like a man who feels at home, shaking a hand here, another one there.

When he felt sure that the interrogation was under way, he went up to the magistrates' corridor and knocked at Dossin's door.

"May I?"

"Come in, Chief Inspector."

A man had risen to his feet, small and very slim, too

deliberately well dressed, whom Maigret instantly recognized from his photographs in the papers. He had
put on a pompous manner in order to look older, af-
fecting a self-assurance that did not match his age.

Quite handsome, with a sallow complexion and black
hair, he had long nostrils, which quivered from time to
time, and he stared people in the eye as though determined to make them look away.

"Monsieur Maigret, I suppose."

"Yes, indeed, Maître Liotard."

"If you're looking for me, I'll be glad to see you after
the interrogation."

Frans Steuvels, who had remained seated, facing the
judge, was waiting. He had merely glanced at the chief
inspector, then at the police stenographer at the end of
the desk, who still had his pen in his hand.

"I'm not looking for you particularly. I'm looking for
a chair, believe it or not."

He picked one up by its back and straddled it, still
smoking his pipe.

"Do you intend to stay here?"

"Unless Judge Dossin asks me to leave."

"Do stay, Maigret."

"I protest. If the interrogation is going to be conducted
in these circumstances, I object strenuously on the
grounds that the presence of a member of the police in
this office obviously tends to influence my client."

Maigret refrained from muttering: "Get it off your
chest, my boy."

He watched the young lawyer with an ironic expression. Liotard obviously didn't believe a word he was saying. It was part of his strategy. At every interrogation so
far, he had precipitated a confrontation, for the most
futile or extravagant reason.

"There is no regulation that prevents an officer of the Police Judiciaire from being present at an interrogation. So, if you don't mind, we'll go on where we left off."

Yet Dossin was himself influenced by Maigret's presence, and he took a while to find his place in his notes.

"I asked you, Steuvels, if you are in the habit of buying your clothes ready-made or if you have a tailor."

"It depends," the prisoner replied, after reflecting.

"On what?"

"I hardly bother about clothes at all. When I need a suit, I sometimes get it ready-made, but I've also had them made for me."

"By which tailor?"

"I had a suit made several years ago by a neighbor, a Polish Jew, who has since disappeared. . . . I think he went to America."

"Was it a blue suit?"

"No. It was gray."

"How long did you wear it?"

"Two or three years. . . . I forget."

"And your blue suit?"

"It must be ten years since I bought a blue suit."

"But the neighbors saw you dressed in blue not long ago."

"They must have confused my suit with my coat."

It was true that a navy-blue overcoat had been found in the apartment.

"When did you buy this coat?"

"Last winter."

"Isn't it unlikely that you would buy a blue coat if your only suit was brown? The two colors don't go together particularly well."

"I'm not fashionable."

All this time, Liotard stared at Maigret with a look of

defiance so intense that he seemed to be trying to hypnotize him. Then, just as he would have done in court, to impress the jury, he shrugged his shoulders, smiled sarcastically.

"Why don't you admit that the suit found in the closet belongs to you?"

"Because it doesn't."

"How do you account for someone having managed to place it there, seeing that you almost never leave your home, and your bedroom can be reached only by going through the workshop?"

"I don't explain it."

"Let's be reasonable, Monsieur Steuvels. I'm not trying to trap you. This is the third time at least that we've discussed this subject. According to you, somebody entered your home, unknown to you, to place two human teeth in the ashes of your furnace. Note that this person chose the day when your wife was absent, and that in order to make sure she would be absent he had to go to Concarneau—or send an accomplice—to dispatch a telegram about her mother's illness. . . . That's not all!

"Not only were you alone at home, which is hardly ever the case, but, furthermore, that night you had such a big fire going in your furnace that it took you several trips to carry the ashes out to the ash cans.

"On this point we have the evidence of your concierge, Madame Salazar, who has no reason to lie and who is in a good position, in her lodge, to keep an eye on the comings and goings of her tenants. On Sunday morning, she says, you made at least five trips, each time with a big bucket full of ashes.

"She thought you had been doing some spring cleaning, burning old papers.

"We have more evidence, from Mademoiselle Béguin,

68

who lives on the fifth floor and who states that your chimney smoked incessantly all day Sunday. Black smoke, she specifies. At one point she opened her window and noticed an unpleasant smell."

"Is it not a fact that the old lady, Madame Béguin, who is sixty-eight, is generally regarded as not quite all there?" Liotard interrupted, crushing out his cigarette in an ashtray and taking another from a silver case. "May I also point out that for four days, as the weather reports for February 15, 16, 17, and 18 prove, the temperature in Paris and its surroundings was abnormally low?"

"That doesn't explain the teeth. Neither does it explain the presence of the blue suit in the closet, or the bloodstains on it."

"You're making the charge, and it's up to you to prove it. But you're not able to prove that the suit actually belongs to my client."

"May I ask a question, Judge?"

The examining magistrate turned to the lawyer, who had no time to protest. Maigret, turning to face the man from Flanders, was already speaking:

"When did you first hear of Maître Philippe Liotard?"

The lawyer stood up to answer, but Maigret, unperturbed, went on:

"When I finished questioning you on the night of your arrest—or, rather, in the early hours of the morning—and asked you if you wanted the services of a lawyer, you answered affirmatively and named Liotard."

"The prisoner has a perfect right to choose any lawyer he likes, and if this question is asked again, I shall be obliged to bring the matter up before the Bar Association."

"Go ahead. Go ahead and bring it up. . . . It's you I'm talking to, Steuvels. You haven't answered me.

"It wouldn't have been at all surprising if you had mentioned the name of a well-known counsel or lawyer, but that's not the case.

"In my office you didn't consult any directory; you didn't ask anybody any questions.

"Liotard doesn't live in your neighborhood. I believe that until three weeks ago his name had never appeared in the paper."

"I protest."

"Protest all you like . . . As for you, Steuvels, tell me whether, on the morning of the twenty-first, before my inspector's visit, you had ever heard of Maître Liotard. If you had, tell me when and where."

"Don't answer."

The man from Flanders hesitated. His back was hunched and he watched Maigret through his thick glasses.

"You refuse to answer? . . . All right. I'll ask you something else. Did you receive a telephone call on that same day, the twenty-first, during the afternoon, about Maître Liotard?"

Steuvels still hesitated.

"Or, if you prefer, did you call anybody? I'm going to take you back to the atmosphere of that day, which had begun just like any other day. The sun was shining, and it was very mild, so you hadn't started the furnace. You were at work, facing your window, when my inspector appeared and asked to see your premises, on some pretext."

"So you admit that!" interrupted Liotard.

"I admit it, Maître. . . . It's not you I'm interrogating, however.

"You immediately realized that the police had their eye on you, Steuvels.

"At that time, there was a reddish-brown suitcase in your workshop, which was gone when Inspector Lucas came later with a search warrant.

"Who phoned you? Or whom did you warn? Who came to see you between the visits of Lapointe and Lucas? . . .

"I've had a check made of the people you call frequently, whose numbers you'd written down on a pad. I checked your telephone directory myself. Liotard's name does not appear among those of your clients either.

"Yet he came to see you that day. Did you send for him, or did someone you know send him to you?"

"I forbid you to answer."

But the man from Flanders made a gesture of impatience.

"He came on his own."

"You are referring to Maître Liotard, aren't you?"

The bookbinder looked at each of the men around him, and his eyes shone as if he took personal delight in putting his lawyer in an embarrassing position.

"Yes. Maître Liotard."

The lawyer turned to the police stenographer and said:

"You have no right to put these answers on record. They have nothing to do with the case. . . . I did, in fact, go to see Steuvels, whose reputation was known to me, to ask him if he could do a binding job for me. Is that so?"

"That's so."

Why in the world was a malicious little spark dancing in the bright pupils of Steuvels' eyes?

"It was about a bookplate with the family coat of arms. Oh, yes, Monsieur Maigret, my grandfather was known

71

as Comte de Liotard; he voluntarily stopped using his title when he lost all his money. I wanted a family coat of arms and went to Steuvels, the best bookbinder in Paris, though I had been told he was terribly busy."

"You didn't talk to him about anything besides your coat of arms?"

"I beg your pardon, but it seems to me that you are now interrogating me. . . . This is your office, Judge Dossin, and I do not wish to be called to account by a member of the police. Even when it was my client who was concerned, I had serious objections. But for a member of the bar . . ."

"Have you any other questions to put to Steuvels, Chief Inspector?"

"No more, thank you."

It was strange. It still seemed as though the bookbinder was not annoyed at what had happened and that he was looking at Maigret with newfound liking.

As for the lawyer, he had sat down again and picked up a file, in which he pretended to be absorbed.

"You can find me any time you want me, Maître Liotard. Do you know my office? The next to the last on the left, at the end of the corridor."

He smiled at Dossin, who was feeling somewhat uncomfortable, and walked toward the little door that connects the Police Judiciaire with the Palais de Justice.

The PJ was more of a beehive than ever: telephones in use behind every door, people waiting in every corner, inspectors rushing up and down the corridors.

"I think there's someone waiting for you in your office, Chief Inspector."

When he pushed the door open, he found Fernande with Lapointe, who, sitting in Maigret's place, was listening to her and taking notes. The inspector stood up in some confusion.

The bookbinder's wife was wearing a beige gabardine raincoat and a hat of the same material, quite without style.

"How is he?" she asked. "Have you seen him? Is he still up there?"

"He's getting on well. He admits that Liotard called at his workshop on the afternoon of the twenty-first."

"A more disturbing thing has just happened," she said. "Please, please take what I'm about to tell you seriously. . . . This morning I left as usual to take his dinner to Santé. You know the little enamel casseroles I put it in? . . .

"I took the Métro at Saint-Paul and changed at Châtelet. I bought a paper on the way, because I hadn't had time to read one at home, and I sat down in a seat near the door and began the article—you know the one I mean.

"I had put the stack of casseroles on the floor beside me, and I could feel the heat from them against my leg.

"There must have been a train departure soon, because a few stops before Montparnasse a lot of people got into the car, and a good many of them had suitcases.

"I was busy reading and not paying attention to what was going on around me. Suddenly I had the feeling that someone was touching my casseroles.

"I just had time to see a hand trying to put the metal handle back in position.

"I stood up and turned to face the person next to me. We were pulling into Montparnasse, where I had to change. Nearly everybody was getting out.

"I don't know how he did it, but he managed to upset

73

the whole thing and make his way out to the platform before I could see him full face.

"The food spilled all over the place. . . . I've brought you the casseroles, which are almost empty, except for the bottom one.

"Look at them for yourself. A strip of metal with a handle on top holds them together. It can't open by itself. I'm sure somebody was following me and tried to slip poison into the food meant for Frans."

"Take it to the lab," Maigret said to Lapointe.

"They may not find anything, because, of course, it was the top one he tried to put the poison in, and it's empty. Can't you believe me just the same, Chief Inspector? You must know that I've been honest with you."

"Always?"

"As far as possible. This time Frans's life is at stake. Somebody's trying to get rid of him, and the dirty crook wanted to use me without my knowing it."

Her bitterness was brimming over.

"If only I hadn't been so absorbed in the paper, I might have had a good look at the man. The only thing I know is that he was wearing a raincoat about the same color as mine, and his black shoes were worn."

"Young?"

"Not very. Not old either. Middle-aged. Or a man of no particular age, if you know what I mean. There was a stain near the shoulder of his raincoat. I noticed it while he was getting off."

"Tall? Slender?"

"Rather small. Average height, at the most. Looked like a rat, if you want my opinion."

"And you're sure you've never seen him before?"

She thought for a moment.

"No. He doesn't suggest anything."

Then, changing her mind:

"Now it's coming back to me. I was just reading the piece about the woman with the little boy at the Hotel Beauséjour. He reminded me of one of those two men, the one the proprietress said looked like the type that sells fancy postcards. . . . You're not laughing at me, are you?"

"No."

"You don't think I'm making it all up?"

"No."

"Do you think somebody's trying to kill him?"

"Possibly."

"What are you going to do?"

"I don't know yet."

Lapointe came back to say that the laboratory could not let them have a report for several hours.

"Do you think he'd better stick to prison food?"

"It would be safer."

"He'll be wondering why I haven't sent his meal. And I won't see him for two days, not until visiting time."

She wasn't crying or making a fuss, but her dull eyes, deeply ringed, were full of anxiety and distress.

"Come with me."

He winked at Lapointe, led her downstairs, through corridors that became more and more deserted the farther they went. With some trouble, he opened a little window overlooking the courtyard, where a Black Maria was waiting.

"He'll be down in a minute. Will you excuse me? There's something I must attend to. . . ."

He made a gesture toward the upper floor.

Surprised, she watched him. Then she took hold of the bars with both hands, and leaned out as far as possible, looking in the direction from which Steuvels would emerge.

Something about a Hat

It was restful, after leaving the office, where doors banged incessantly behind inspectors and where all the telephones were ringing simultaneously, to make his way, via a usually deserted staircase, up to the top floor of the Palais de Justice, where the Forensic Laboratory and Criminal Records were located.

It was nearly dark outside, and in the badly lighted stairwell, which was like some secret staircase in a castle, Maigret was preceded by his gigantic shadow.

In a corner under the mansard roof, Moers, a green eyeshade above his thick spectacles, was working under a lamp that he could move closer to or farther away from his work by pulling on a wire.

This man had not been to Rue de Turenne to question the residents or to drink Pernod and white wine in one of the three cafés. He had never followed anyone in the

76

street or spent the night in some hidden place outside a closed door.

He never got upset or nervous, yet quite likely tomorrow morning would find him still hunched over his desk. Once, he had spent three consecutive days and nights at it.

Maigret, without saying a word, picked up a cane-bottomed chair, sat down near the inspector, and lighted his pipe, on which he puffed gently. Hearing a rhythmic sound on a skylight above his head, he knew that the weather had changed, and it had begun to rain.

"Look at these, Chief," Moers said, handing him three stacks of photographs.

He had turned out a magnificent job, all by himself in his hideaway. From the vague specifications he had been given, he had somehow brought to life and endowed with personality three people of whom almost nothing was known: the fat, dark foreigner with the elegant clothes; the young woman with the white hat; the accomplice who looked like a man who sells "fancy postcards."

To achieve this, he had at his disposal hundreds of thousands of record cards, but he was certainly the only person who carried in his head sufficient knowledge of the data contained on them to be capable of accomplishing what he had.

The first batch Maigret examined contained many photographs of stout, well-groomed men, Greek or Levantine, with sleek hair and rings on their fingers.

"I'm not too pleased with those." Moers sighed, as if he were faced with selecting the ideal cast for a film. "But you can give them a try anyhow. . . . I like these better."

There were only about fifteen in the second batch, and every one made Maigret feel like applauding, because they bore so close a resemblance to his mental picture of the person described by the proprietress of the Beauséjour.

Turning them over, he learned the profession of each subject. Two or three were racetrack touts. There was a pickpocket who was especially familiar to him, because he had personally arrested him in a bus, and an individual who hung around outside big hotels soliciting business for "specialized" establishments.

A satisfied little spark was dancing in Moers's eyes.

"It's amusing, isn't it, that I've got hardly anything on the woman. That's because our photos never show hats. But I'll keep at it."

Maigret, who had slipped the photographs into his pocket, stayed a few minutes longer, just because he felt like it. Then, with a sigh, he went into the laboratory next door, where they were still working on the food in Fernande's casseroles.

They hadn't found anything. Either the story was a complete fabrication, for some purpose he couldn't guess, or there hadn't been time to introduce the poison, or it had been in the portion that had been spilled in the Métro car.

Maigret, avoiding a return through the PJ offices, went out into the rain on Quai des Orfèvres, turned up his coat collar, and walked toward Pont Saint-Michel. He had to hail about ten taxis before one stopped.

"Place Blanche. Corner of Rue Lepic."

He felt out of sorts, dissatisfied with himself and with the way the case was going. He was particularly resentful of Philippe Liotard, who had forced him to abandon his usual methods and mobilize all the various PJ divisions right at the start.

Now, too many people he couldn't control personally

78

were mixed up in the case. And it seemed to be getting more and more complicated, all by itself; new characters were popping up about whom he knew almost nothing and whose roles he couldn't guess.

Twice he had been tempted to go back to the very beginning of the inquiry by himself, and work slowly, deliberately, using his favorite method. But this was no longer possible; the machine was running, and there was no way to stop it.

He would have liked, for instance, to question the concierge, the shoemaker across the street, the old maid on the fifth floor. But what was the use? Everybody had questioned them by now—inspectors, reporters, amateur detectives, people in the street. Their statements had been published in the papers, and they couldn't go back on them now. It was like a trail that has been heedlessly trampled on by fifty people.

"Do you think the bookbinder murdered someone, Monsieur Maigret?"

It was the driver, who had recognized him and was questioning him as if they were on familiar terms.

"I don't know."

"If I were you, I'd pay particular attention to the little boy. That seems to be the best lead. And I'm not saying that just because I have one his age."

Even the taxi drivers were getting into it!

He went into the bar on the corner of Rue Lepic for a drink. Big drops of rain were dripping from the awning around the terrace, where a few women were sitting, as rigid as waxworks. He knew most of them. Some probably took their clients to the Hotel Beauséjour.

There was one—very fat—blocking the doorway of the hotel as he approached. She smiled, thinking he wanted her, then recognized him and apologized.

He went up the badly lighted stairs, found the proprietress in the office, dressed this time in black silk and wearing gold-rimmed spectacles. Her hair was a flaming red.

"Sit down. Excuse me a moment, will you? . . . A towel for Number 17, Emma!"

She came back.

"Have you found out anything new?"

"I'd like you to examine these pictures carefully."

He handed her the photographs of women that Moers had picked out. She looked at them one by one, shook her head every time, and passed them back to him.

"No. They're not the type at all. She's more refined than these women. . . . Perhaps not exactly refined. What I mean is respectable. Do you know what I'm getting at? . . . She looks like a decent little woman, but these might be women who come to this hotel."

"What about these?"

As she looked at the dark-haired men, she shook her head.

"No. They're not right at all. I don't know how to explain to you. These look too much like dagos. Monsieur Levine could have stayed at a big hotel on the Champs-Elysées without looking out of place."

"And these?"

He handed her the last batch.

The minute she came to the third photograph, she stiffened and cast a furtive glance at the chief inspector. Why was she reluctant to speak out?

"Is that the other man?"

"It may be. Wait till I take it to the light."

A girl was coming upstairs with a client, who kept to the darkest part of the staircase.

"Take Number 7, Clémence. The room's just been done."

She shifted her spectacles on her nose.

"I'd swear it's him. Yes. It's too bad he can't move. If I saw his walk, even from behind, I'd know him at once. . . . But it's very unlikely that I'm wrong."

On the back of the photograph, Moers had written a résumé of what was known about the man. Maigret noted with interest that he was probably a Belgian, like the bookbinder. "Probably" because he was known under several different names, and his true identity had never been established.

"Thank you."

"I hope you'll give me credit for this. I could very well have pretended not to recognize him. After all, they may be dangerous, and I'm taking a big risk."

She reeked so strongly of scent, and the odors in the house were so clinging, that he was glad to be back on the sidewalk breathing the smell of rain-washed streets.

It was not yet seven o'clock. Lapointe must have gone to meet his sister and tell her what had happened at the PJ that day, just as Maigret had advised him to. He was a good boy, too easily upset, too emotional, but they could probably make something of him.

Lucas, in his office, was still acting as orchestra conductor, keeping in touch by telephone with all divisions, all sections of Paris, and anywhere else the trio might be found.

As for Janvier, he was sticking to Alfonsi, who had gone back to Rue de Turenne and stayed nearly an hour in the basement with Fernande.

The chief inspector drank another glass of beer while he read the notes written by Moers, which reminded him of something, but what?

> Alfred Moss. Belgian nationality (?). About 42. Vaude-
> ville artiste for about ten years. Member of acrobatic act
> on horizontal bars: Moss, Jeff, and Joe.

Maigret was remembering now. He was remembering particularly the one man of the three who played the clown, in baggy black clothes and enormous shoes, with a blue chin, a huge red mouth, and a green wig.

The man seemed to be completely disjointed, and after each leap he would pretend to fall so heavily that it seemed impossible he hadn't broken something.

> Has worked in most countries of Europe and in the
> United States, where he was with Ringling Brothers' Cir-
> cus for four years. Retired after an accident.

Then followed the names by which he had been known to the police since then: Mosselaer, Van Vlanderen, Paterson, Smith, Thomas . . . He had been arrested successively in Manchester, Brussels, Amsterdam, and three or four times in Paris.

He had never been convicted, however, for lack of proof. Whichever identity he was using, his papers were invariably in order, and he spoke four or five languages perfectly enough to change his nationality whenever it suited him.

The first time he had been prosecuted was in London, where he claimed to be a Swiss citizen and worked as an interpreter in a classy hotel. A jewel case had disappeared from a suite he had been seen leaving, but the owner of the jewels, an elderly American woman, testified that she herself had summoned him to the suite, to translate a letter she had received from Germany.

In Amsterdam, four years later, he had been suspected

of being a con man. Proof could not be established, any more than it could the first time. Then he disappeared from circulation for a while.

The police division in charge of national surveillance, the DST, was the next to take an interest in him, again unsuccessfully, during a period when there was large-scale traffic in gold across French borders, and when Moss, as Joseph Thomas, was shuttling between France and Belgium.

He had his ups and downs, living now in a first-class, sometimes even a deluxe, hotel and sometimes in a shabby furnished room.

For three years there had been no record of him anywhere. It was not known in what country or under what name he was operating, assuming that he was still operating.

Maigret walked toward a telephone booth and got Lucas on the phone.

"Go up and see Moers and ask him for all the information on a man named Moss. . . . Yes. Tell him he's one of the group. He'll give you his description and all the rest of it. Put out a general alert. He's not to be arrested. If he's found, his suspicion should not be aroused. Get it?"

"I get it, Chief. . . . Someone's just spotted the child again."

"Where?"

"Avenue Denfert-Rochereau. I've sent someone over. . . . I haven't got enough men available right now. There's also been a call from the Gare du Nord. Torrence has gone there."

He felt like walking in the rain and went through Place d'Anvers, where he looked at the bench, now dripping, where Madame Maigret had waited. Opposite, on the building at the corner of Avenue Trudaine, was a sign, in big, faded letters: *Dentist*.

He would come back. There were so many things he wanted to do that the pressure always forced him to postpone to another day.

He jumped on a bus. When he arrived at his own door, he was surprised not to hear any sound from the kitchen, not to smell anything cooking. He entered, went through the dining room, where the table wasn't set, and finally saw Madame Maigret, in her slip, taking off her stockings.

This was so unlike her that he didn't know what to say, and she burst out laughing when she saw his big round eyes.

"Are you cross, Maigret?"

Her voice held a tone of almost aggressive good humor, which was quite new to him. On the bed he could see her best dress and her Sunday hat.

"You'll have to be content with a cold dinner. Just imagine, I've been so busy that I haven't had time to prepare anything. Besides, you so seldom come home to meals nowadays!"

Sitting in her easy chair, she rubbed her feet with a sigh of relief.

"I think I've never walked so much in my life!"

He stood there in his coat, with his wet hat on his head, looking at her and waiting. She was deliberately keeping him on tenterhooks.

"I began with the big stores, although I was almost sure that was no use. But you never know, and I didn't want to regret my carelessness later. . . . Then I did the whole of Rue Lafayette. I went up Rue Notre-Dame-de-Lorette and walked along Rue Blanche and Rue de Clichy. I came back down toward the Opéra. All this on foot, even after it had begun to rain. . . . I suppose I may as well admit that yesterday, without telling you, I did the Ternes area and the Champs-Elysées . . . just to make absolutely sure, though I suspected that it was too expensive around there."

At last he brought out the sentence she was waiting for, which she'd been trying to elicit.

"What were you looking for?"

"The hat, of course! Didn't you catch on? . . . It was on my mind, that business. I thought it wasn't a man's job. A suit is a suit, especially a blue one. But a hat— that's different. And I'd had a good look at this one. They've been wearing white hats for several weeks now. Only, one hat is never exactly like another. Do you see? . . . You don't mind if dinner's cold, do you? I brought in some cold things from the Italian place—Parma ham, pickled mushrooms, and a lot of ready-to-eat hors d'oeuvres."

"What about the hat?"

"Are you interested in it, Maigret? . . . By the way, your own is dripping on the carpet. You'd better take it off."

She had been successful—otherwise she wouldn't be in such a teasing mood and would never take the liberty of playing with him like this. He would just have to let her take her time and maintain his grouchy expression, because she was enjoying it.

While she was putting on a woolen dress, he sat on the edge of the bed.

"I knew it wasn't a hat from a really first-class milliner, and that there was no sense in looking on Rue de la Paix, Rue Saint-Honoré, or Avenue Matignon. Anyhow, those places don't put anything in the window, and I'd have had to go in and pretend to be a customer. Can you see me trying on hats at Caroline Reboux or Rose Valois? . . .

"But it wasn't a hat from the Galeries or Printemps either.

"Somewhere between the two. A hat from a milliner's definitely, and a milliner with good taste.

"That's why I did all the little shops, especially around Place d'Anvers—or not too far away.

"I saw at least a hundred white hats. Yet it was a pearl-gray one that finally stopped me. On Rue Caumartin, at Hélène and Rosine's.

"It was exactly the same hat, in another shade, and I'm sure I'm not mistaken. I told you that the one belonging to the nice lady with the little boy had a tiny veil, three or four fingers wide, that came down just over the eyes.

"The gray hat had the same veil."

"Did you go in?"

Maigret had to make an effort not to smile. It was the first time that shy Madame Maigret had taken part in an investigation, and no doubt also the first time she had entered a milliner's in the neighborhood of the Opéra.

"Are you surprised? Do you think I look too much of a homebody? . . . Yes, I did go in. I was afraid it might be closed later. I asked perfectly naturally if they had the same hat in white.

"The saleslady said no, but they had it in pale blue, yellow, and jade green. She added that they had had it in white, but they had sold that one more than a month ago."

"What did you do?" he asked, intrigued.

"I heaved a deep sigh and said to her: 'That must have been the one I saw a friend of mine wearing.'

"I could see myself—because there are mirrors all around the shop—and my face was scarlet.

" 'Do you know Countess Panetti?' she asked, and her astonishment wasn't very complimentary.

" 'I've met her. . . . I'd very much like to see her again, because I have information for her that she asked me to try to get. But I've mislaid her address.'

" 'I suppose she'd still at . . .'

"She was on the point of stopping there, not being completely sure of me. But she couldn't very well not finish her sentence.

" 'I suppose she's still at the Claridge.' "

Madame Maigret was looking at him triumphantly and teasingly at the same time, but with an anxious trembling of her lips in spite of that. He kept up the game, and muttered:

"I hope you didn't go interrogating the bell captain at the Claridge."

"I came straight back. Are you cross?"

"No."

"I've caused you enough trouble with this business. The least I can do is try to help you. . . . Now come and eat. I hope you're going to take time for a bite before you go over there."

This dinner reminded him of their first meals together, when she was discovering Paris and was delighted by all the little ready-to-eat items sold in the Italian shops. It was more like a picnic than a dinner.

"Do you think the information's reliable?"

"So long as you didn't get the wrong hat."

"I'm absolutely sure about that. As far as the shoes go, I'm not so confident."

"What's this about shoes now?"

"When you're sitting on a park bench, your eyes naturally fall on the shoes of the person next to you. Once, when I looked at them closely, I could see that she was embarrassed and was trying to stick her feet under the bench."

"Why?"

"I'll explain, Maigret. Don't make that face! It's not your fault if you don't know everything about female behavior. . . . Suppose someone accustomed to first-class couturiers wants to look like a little housewife and be inconspicuous. She buys a ready-made suit, which is easy. She may also buy a hat that isn't deluxe class, although I'm not quite so sure about the hat."

"What do you mean?"

"She may already have had it and thought it looked enough like the other white hats being worn this season by shopgirls. She takes off her jewelry, certainly. But there's one thing she would have a lot of trouble getting used to: ready-made shoes. Having your shoes custom-made by the best bootmakers gives you delicate feet. You've heard me groaning often enough to know that women have sensitive feet by nature. So she keeps her own shoes, thinking no one will notice them. That's where she's wrong. As far as I'm concerned, that's the first thing I look at. Usually it happens the other way around: you see pretty, well-dressed women with expensive outfits or fur coats wearing cheap shoes."

"Did she have expensive shoes?"

"Custom-made, I'm sure. I don't know enough about them to say where they came from. No doubt some women could have told."

He took time after dinner to pour himself a little glass of prunelle and to smoke almost a whole pipe.

"Are you going to the Claridge? You won't be too late?"

He took a taxi, got out opposite the luxury hotel on

the Champs-Elysées, and walked over to the bell captain's nook. It was the night man by this time, one he'd known for years. This was good, because night bell captains invariably know more about guests than those on the day shift.

His arrival in a place like this always produced the same effect. He could see the clerks at the reception desk, the assistant manager, and even the elevator boys raising their eyebrows and wondering what was up. Scandals are unpopular in luxury hotels, and the presence of a chief inspector from the Police Judiciaire rarely bodes good.

"How are you, Benoît?"

"Not too bad, Monsieur Maigret. . . . The Americans are beginning to show up."

"Is Countess Panetti still here?"

"No. It's at least a month since she left. Would you like me to check the exact date?"

"Did her family go with her?"

"What family?"

It was a slack time. Most of the guests were out, at the theater or dinner. In the golden light, the bellboys, their arms dangling, stood near the marble columns and watched the chief inspector, whom they all knew by sight, at least from a distance.

"I never knew she had any family. She's been staying here for years now, and—"

"Tell me, have you ever seen the countess in a white hat?"

"Certainly. She received one a few days before she left."

"Did she also wear a blue suit?"

"No. You must have got them mixed up, Monsieur

Maigret. The blue suit is her maid's, or her companion's, if you prefer it. In any case, it belongs to the young woman who travels with her."

"You've never seen Countess Panetti in a blue suit?"

"If you knew her, you wouldn't ask that."

Just on the chance, Maigret handed him the photographs of the women picked out by Moers.

"Anyone there who looks like her?"

Benoît stared at the chief inspector, flabbergasted.

"You're on the wrong track. These are women under thirty, and the countess isn't much less than seventy. . . . Listen, you'd better find out what your colleagues on the Morals Squad have on her, because they must know her. . . .

"We get all kinds, don't we? Oh, well! The countess is one of our most unusual guests."

"In the first place, who is she?"

"She's the widow of Count Panetti, that munitions and heavy-industry man in Italy. She lives all over the place—Paris, Cannes, Egypt. I think she spends some time every year in Vichy too."

"Does she drink?"

"Shall we say she uses champagne instead of water? I wouldn't be surprised if she brushed her teeth with Pommery brut! She dresses like a young girl, makes up like a doll, and spends most of every night in clubs."

"Her maid?"

"I don't know much about her. She's always getting new ones. . . . I haven't seen this one until this year. Last year, she had a big girl with red hair, a professional masseuse, because she used to like a massage every day."

"Do you know the girl's name?"

"Gloria something. I haven't got her slip anymore, but

they'll have it in the office. I don't know if she's Italian or just from the South, possibly Toulouse."

"Small and dark?"

"Yes. Well dressed, well mannered, pretty. I didn't see much of her. She lived in the suite, not in a servant's room, and she had her meals with her employer."

"No man?"

"Only the son-in-law, who came to see the countess from time to time."

"When?"

"Not long before they left. Ask the desk for the dates. He didn't live in the hotel."

"Do you know his name?"

"Krynker, I think. He's Czech or Hungarian."

"Dark, rather heavy, around forty?"

"No. Very fair and much younger. I doubt he's more than thirty."

They were interrupted by a group of American women in evening dress who deposited their keys and asked for a taxi.

"As for swearing that he was really a son-in-law . . ."

"Did she have affairs?"

"I don't know. I can't answer yes or no."

"Did the son-in-law ever spend the night here?"

"No. But they went out together several times."

"With the companion?"

"She never went out at night with the countess. I've never even seen her in evening dress."

"Do you know where they went?"

"The Riviera maybe. . . . Just a minute. Something's come back to me. . . . Ernest! Come here. There's nothing to be afraid of. Didn't Countess Panetti leave her trunks behind?"

"Yes, sir."

The bell captain explained:

"Our clients often, when they're going to be away for a fairly long time, leave some of their luggage here. We have a special baggage room for it."

"She didn't say when she would be back?"

"Not that I know of."

"Did she leave alone?"

"With her maid."

"In a taxi?"

"You'd have to ask my opposite number on the day shift about that. You'll find him here tomorrow morning from eight o'clock on."

Maigret took the photograph of Moss out of his pocket.

The bell captain merely glanced at it and made a face. "You won't find *him* here," he said.

"Do you know him?"

"Paterson. I knew him, under the name Mosselaer, when I was working in Milan, at least fifteen years ago. He's barred from all the luxury hotels, and he wouldn't dare show his face here. He knows none of them would give him a room, or even allow him to walk across the lobby."

"You haven't seen him recently?"

"No. If I did run into him, I'd start by asking him for the hundred lire he borrowed from me years ago and never returned."

"Does the day man have a telephone?"

"You can try to call him at this place in Saint-Cloud, but he hardly ever answers. He doesn't like to be disturbed in the evening, so he usually takes the phone off the hook."

Nevertheless, he did answer, and the music from his radio was audible over the telephone too.

"The head baggage porter could give you more accurate information, I'm sure. I don't remember having a taxi called for her. Generally, when she leaves, she asks me to get her train or plane tickets."

"You didn't do it this time?"

"No . . . Oh, it's just struck me: maybe she left in a private car."

"Do you know whether the son-in-law, Krynker, owned a car?"

"He certainly did! A big chocolate-colored American one."

"Thank you. I'll probably come see you tomorrow morning."

He went over to the desk, where the assistant manager, in black coat and striped trousers, insisted on finding the slips himself.

"She left the hotel on February 15, during the evening. I have her bill right here."

"Was she alone?"

"I see two luncheons down for that day. So she must have eaten with her companion."

"Would you please lend me the bill?"

It showed the daily expenditures of the countess at the hotel, and Maigret wanted to study them at leisure.

"On condition you give it back to me! Otherwise, we'll be in trouble with the tax fellows. . . . By the way, how do the police come to be interested in a person like Countess Panetti?"

Maigret, his mind on something else, almost replied: "All because of my wife!"

He caught himself in time and muttered:

"I don't know yet. Something about a hat."

The Laundry Boat
on the Seine

Maigret pushed the revolving door, catching sight of the garlands of lights on the Champs-Elysées, which, in the rain, always reminded him of moist eyes. He was about to start walking down to the Rond Point when he raised his eyebrows. Leaning against a tree, not far from a flower girl who was sheltering from the rain, Janvier, pathetic, comical, was looking at him as if he was trying to tell him something.

Maigret walked up to him.

"What in the world are you doing here?"

The inspector indicated a silhouette outlined against one of the few illuminated shopwindows. It was Alfonsi, who seemed intensely interested in a display of luggage.

"He's following you. So that's why I happen to be following you too."

"Did he see Liotard after his visit to Rue de Turenne?"

"No. He phoned him."

"Well, call it a day. Do you want me to drop you home?"

Janvier lived not far out of his way, on Rue Réaumur.

Alfonsi, taken aback, watched them walk off together. When Maigret hailed a taxi, he turned and went off in the direction of the Etoile.

"Anything new?" Janvier asked.

"Any amount. Too much, almost."

"Do you want me to take care of Alfonsi again tomorrow morning?"

"No. Come to the office. There'll probably be plenty of work for everybody."

When the inspector got out, Maigret said to the driver:

"Go down Rue de Turenne."

It wasn't late. He vaguely hoped he would see a light at the bookbinder's.

This would be the ideal time for the long chat with Fernande he had been hankering after for quite a while.

Because of a reflection on the glass door, he got out of the taxi, but finding the interior dark, hesitated to knock, and set off in the direction of the Quai des Orfèvres. Torrence was on duty, and he gave him some instructions.

Madame Maigret had just gone to bed when he tiptoed in. As he was undressing in the dark, so as not to wake her, she asked:

"The hat?"

"It was bought by Countess Panetti, all right."

"Did you see her?"

"No. But she's about seventy."

He went to bed in a bad temper. And it was still raining when he woke in the morning. Preoccupied, he cut himself while shaving.

"Are you going on with your investigation?" he asked his wife, who, in curlers, was serving his breakfast.

"Is there something else for me to do?" she inquired seriously.

"I don't know. Now that you've started . . ."

He bought his paper at the corner of Boulevard Voltaire, but found no new manifesto by Philippe Liotard, no new challenge. The night bell captain at the Claridge had been discreet; there was no mention of the countess either.

At the PJ, Lucas had relieved Torrence and received Maigret's instructions; the machine was functioning. They were now looking for the Italian countess on the Riviera and in various foreign capitals, while inquiries were also being made about the man named Krynker and the maid.

On the rear platform of the bus, enveloped in fine rain, a passenger facing him was reading his paper, and this paper carried a headline that gave the chief inspector something to think about.

INQUIRY DRAGS

How many people, at that very minute, were actively engaged in it? Railway stations, ports, and airports were still under observation. Hotels and rooming houses were continuously being searched. Not only in Paris, but throughout France, and in London, Brussels, Amsterdam, Rome, they were trying to pick up the track of Alfred Moss.

Maigret got out at Rue de Turenne, entered the Tabac des Vosges to buy some tobacco, and took the opportunity of drinking a glass of white wine. There were no reporters; only local residents, who were beginning to pull in their horns.

The bookbinder's door was locked. He knocked, and soon saw Fernande emerging from the basement by the spiral staircase. In curlers, like Madame Maigret, she hesitated when she recognized him through the glass, but finally opened the door.

"I'd like to talk to you for a few minutes."

It was chilly, since the furnace had not been relighted.

"Wouldn't you rather come downstairs?" she asked.

He followed her into the kitchen, which she had been in the middle of cleaning when he disturbed her.

She, too, seemed tired, and there was something like discouragement in her expression.

"Would you like a cup of coffee? I have some hot."

He accepted and sat down at the table. She sat down facing him, wrapping her bathrobe around her bare legs.

"Alfonsi came to see you yesterday. What does he want?"

"I don't know. He's interested mainly in the questions you ask me, and he keeps telling me not to trust you."

"Did you mention the poisoning attempt to him?"

"Yes."

"Why?"

"You didn't tell me not to. . . . I can't remember how it came up. He's working for Liotard, and it seems all right for him to be kept informed."

"No one else has been to see you?"

It seemed to him that she hesitated, but it may have been the effect of the weariness weighing upon the wife of the man from Flanders. She had helped herself to a big cup of coffee. She probably relied on black coffee in copious amounts to keep her going.

"No. Nobody."

"Did you tell your husband why you're not bringing his meals anymore?"

"I managed to let him know. . . . I appreciate what you did."

"No one's called you?"

"No. I don't think so. I hear the bell occasionally, but by the time I get upstairs there's no one on the line."

He took from his pocket the photograph of Alfred Moss.

"Do you recognize this man?"

She looked at the photograph, then at Maigret, and said, quite naturally:

"Of course."

"Who is it?"

"It's Alfred, my husband's brother."

"Has it been a long time since you've seen him?"

"I hardly ever see him. Sometimes he doesn't come here for more than a year. He lives abroad most of the time."

"Do you know what he does?"

"Not exactly. Frans says he's unfortunate, a failure, who never had a break."

"He never mentioned his profession?"

"I know he worked in a circus. He was an acrobat, but he broke his spine in a fall."

"Since then?"

"He may be some kind of impresario."

"Did you know that he didn't call himself Steuvels, but Moss? Have you ever been told why?"

"Yes."

She was reluctant to go on. She looked at the picture, which Maigret had left on the table near their coffee cups, then got up to turn off the gas under a pan of water.

"I couldn't help guessing part of it. Perhaps if you question Frans, he'll tell you more. You know that their parents were very poor. But that's not the whole story. . . . Actually, his mother was in the business I used to be in—at Gand, or in a shady district just outside the town.

"She drank, into the bargain. I wonder if she wasn't half crazy. She had seven or eight children, and half the time she didn't know who their father was.

"It was Frans who chose the name Steuvels, later. His mother was called Mosselaer."

"Is she dead?"

"I think so. He doesn't like to talk about her."

"Has he kept in touch with his brothers and sisters?"

"I don't think so. Alfred's the only one who comes to see him from time to time, but rarely. He must have his ups and downs, because sometimes he seems prosperous—he's well dressed, gets out of a taxi, and brings presents—other times, he's quite shabby."

"When did you last see him?"

"Let me think. . . . It must be two months ago at least."

"Did he stay to dinner?"

"Yes. He always does."

"Tell me, during these visits did your husband ever try to get rid of you under any pretext?"

"No. Why? . . . They were sometimes in the workshop by themselves, but from down here, when I was cooking, I could hear what they said."

"What did they talk about?"

"Nothing particular. Alfred liked to reminisce about the time when he was an acrobat, and the different countries he'd lived in. He was the one who nearly always mentioned their childhood and their mother. That's where I got the little information I have."

99

"Alfred is the younger, I suppose?"

"Three or four years younger. . . . Afterward, Frans would sometimes walk to the corner with him. That's the only time I wasn't with them."

"They never talked business?"

"Never."

"Alfred never came with friends, male or female?"

"He was always alone. I think he'd been married once. I'm not sure. It seems to me he mentioned it. . . . At least, he'd been in love with a woman, and she'd made him unhappy."

It was warm and quiet in the little kitchen, from which you couldn't see the outside world at all and where the light had to be kept on all day. Maigret would have liked to have Frans Steuvels there facing him and to talk to him as he was talking to his wife.

"You told me last time I was here that your husband almost never went out without you. Yet he went to the bank from time to time."

"I don't call that going out. It's just around the corner. He only had to walk across Place des Vosges."

"Otherwise you were together from morning to night?"

"Just about. I'd go marketing, of course, but always close by. Once in a great while I'd go downtown to do some shopping. I'm not very stylish, as you may have noticed."

"You never went to see relatives?"

"I have only my mother and my sister, in Concarneau. And it took a fake telegram to get me to go and visit them."

It was as though something were bothering Maigret.

"There's no day when you're regularly out?"

"No. . . . Except for washday, of course."

100

"You don't do the washing here?"

"Where could I do it? I'd have to go up to the street floor for water. I couldn't hang the washing in the workshop, and it wouldn't dry in the basement. So, once a week in summer and once a fortnight in winter, I go to the laundry boat on the Seine."

"Whereabouts?"

"Square du Vert-Galant. You know, just below Pont Neuf. It takes me half a day. The next morning I go to fetch the washing, which is dry and ready to iron."

Visibly Maigret was relaxing, smoking his pipe with more pleasure, and his expression had become livelier.

"In fact, one day a week in summer, one day every two weeks in winter, Frans was alone here?"

"Not all day."

"Did you go to the laundry boat in the morning or the afternoon?"

"Afternoon. I tried going in the morning, but it was difficult, on account of the cleaning and cooking."

"Do you have a key to the house?"

"Of course."

"Did you often have to use it?"

"What do you mean?"

"Did it sometimes happen that when you came back, your husband wasn't in the workshop?"

"Hardly ever."

"But it did happen?"

"I think so. Yes."

"Recently?"

She had just thought of it too, for she hesitated.

"The week I went to Concarneau."

"When's your washday?"

"Monday."

"Did he come home long after you?"

"Not long. Maybe an hour."

"Did you ask him where he'd been?"

"I never ask him anything. He's free. It's not my place to ask him questions."

"You don't know whether he left the neighborhood? . . . Weren't you worried?"

"I was at the door when he came back. I saw him get out of the bus on the corner of Francs-Bourgeois."

"The bus coming from downtown or from the Bastille?"

"From downtown."

"As far as I can tell from this photo, the two brothers are the same height."

"Yes. Alfred looks slimmer because he has a thin face, but his body is more muscular. They're not alike in features, except that they both have red hair. But from behind, the resemblance is striking, and I've occasionally got them mixed up."

"The times when you saw Alfred, how was he dressed?"

"That depended. I've told you already."

"Do you think he borrowed money from his brother?"

"I've thought of that, but it doesn't seem very likely. Not in front of me, in any case."

"On his last visit wasn't he wearing a blue suit?"

She looked him in the eye. She had caught on.

"I'm almost sure he was wearing something dark, but gray, rather than blue. When you live by artificial light, you don't pay much attention to colors."

"How did you manage money, you and your husband?"

"What money?"

"Did he give you housekeeping money every month?"

"No. When I ran out, I'd ask him for some."

"He never protested?"

She turned slightly pink.

"He was absentminded. He always thought he'd given me money just the day before. And he'd be astonished and say: 'What, again?' "

"What about your personal things—dresses and hats?"

"I don't spend much. You must know that."

It was her turn to put some questions to him, as if she had been waiting a long time for this moment.

"Listen, Chief Inspector. I'm not very intelligent, but I'm not so stupid either. You've questioned me; your men have questioned me, and the reporters too, not to mention the tradesmen and the neighbors. A young gentleman of seventeen who plays amateur detective even stopped me on the street and asked me some questions he had written down in a little notebook. Once and for all, tell me honestly: Do you think Frans is guilty?"

"Guilty of what?"

"You know perfectly well: of having killed a man and burned the body in the furnace."

He hesitated. He could have given her any answer that came into his head, but he was determined to be honest.

"I have no idea."

"Then why is he being kept in prison?"

"In the first place, that's not my responsibility; it's the examining magistrate's. And then, you mustn't forget that all the circumstantial evidence is against him."

"The teeth!" she flashed, with irony.

"And, above all, the bloodstains on the blue suit. Don't forget the suitcase that vanished either."

"That I never saw!"

"That doesn't make any difference. Other people saw it—at least my inspector did. And there's the fact that

103

you were called out of town, as if by chance, at that very moment, by a fake telegram. Now, between you and me, I admit that if it were up to me, I'd prefer to let your husband go, but I'd hesitate to release him, for the sake of his own safety. You know what happened yesterday."

"Yes. That's just what I'm thinking about."

"Whether he's guilty or innocent, he seems to be in somebody's way."

"Why did you bring me the photo of his brother?"

"Because, in spite of what you think, that man is quite a dangerous criminal."

"Has he committed murder?"

"Probably not. That type of man hardly ever kills. But he's wanted by the police of three or four countries, and for more than fifteen years he's been living by stealing and swindling. Are you surprised?"

"No."

"Did you suspect it?"

"When Frans told me his brother was unfortunate, it seemed to me that he wasn't using the word 'unfortunate' in its usual sense. Do you think that Alfred would have been capable of kidnapping a child?"

"As I said, I have no idea. . . . By the way, have you ever heard of Countess Panetti?"

"Who's she?"

"A very rich Italian woman who stays at the Claridge."

"Has she been killed too?"

"It's possible, and it's also possible that she's simply spending the carnival season in Cannes or Nice. I'll probably know tonight. . . . I'd like to take another look at your husband's accounts."

"Come upstairs. . . . I have loads of questions to ask you, but they've slipped my mind. It's when you're not here that I think of them. I ought to write them down, like the young man playing detective."

She let him precede her upstairs, then took from a shelf a big black book, which the police had examined five or six times already.

At the very end, an index contained the names of the bookbinder's clients, old and new, in alphabetical order. The name Panetti was not listed. Neither was Krynker.

Steuvels had fine, spiky handwriting. Some letters overlapped others, and he had a peculiar way of making the r's and t's.

"Have you ever heard the name Krynker?"

"Not that I remember . . . Look, we would be together the whole day, but I never assumed the right to ask him questions. Sometimes you seem to forget, Chief Inspector, that I'm not just an ordinary wife. Remember where he found me. What he did has always amazed me. Now, it's suddenly occurred to me, as a result of our conversation, that the reason may be that he remembered what his mother had been."

Maigret seemed no longer to be listening. He strode toward the door, flung it open, and seized Alfonsi by the collar of his camel-hair coat.

"Come here, you. You're at it again. Have you decided to spend your days dogging my heels?"

The man tried to brazen it out, but the chief inspector had a strong grip on his neck and was shaking him like a puppet.

"What are you doing here? You'd better tell me."

"I was waiting for you to leave."

"To pester this woman?"

"I have a right to. Provided she chooses to receive me."

"What are you after?"

"Ask Maître Liotard."

"The hell with Liotard! Let me tell you one thing: If I catch you following me again, I'll have you picked up for living off a prostitute. Understand?"

This wasn't an empty threat. Maigret knew very well that the woman Alfonsi lived with spent most of her evenings in Montmartre nightclubs and that she was not unwilling to accompany visiting foreigners to their hotels.

When he came back to Fernande, he looked relieved, having seen the figure of the private detective making off in the rain toward Place des Vosges.

"What sort of questions does he ask you?"

"Always the same. He wants to know what you ask me, what I've told you, what you're interested in, what objects you've examined."

"I think he'll let you alone in future."

"Do you think Maître Liotard is bad for my husband?"

"Whether he is or not, we can't do anything about it at this point."

He had to go back downstairs, because he'd left the photograph of Moss on the kitchen table. Then, instead of making for Quai des Orfèvres, he crossed the street and entered the shoemaker's shop.

At nine in the morning, the man already had several drinks under his belt and reeked of wine.

"Well, Chief Inspector, everything going all right?"

The two shops were exactly opposite one another. The shoemaker and the bookbinder, both hunched over their work, with only the width of the street between them, could not help seeing each other every time they raised their eyes.

"Can you remember some of the bookbinder's clients?"

"A few. Yes."

"This one?"

He held the photograph under his nose, while Fernande, opposite, watched them anxiously.

"I call him the clown."

"Why?"

"I don't know. Because I think he looks like a clown."

Suddenly he scratched his head, then seemed to make a welcome discovery.

"Look here, stand me a drink, and I'll make it worth your while. It was really good luck that you showed me that picture. I mentioned a clown, and all of a sudden the word made me think of a suitcase. Why? Well, obviously because clowns usually come into the ring with a suitcase."

"You mean the stooges, don't you?"

"Stooges or clowns, it's the same thing. How about a drink?"

"Later."

"You don't trust me? . . . You're wrong. Honest as a newborn babe—that's what I always say. Well, anyhow, there's no doubt that the fellow with the suitcase is your man."

"What fellow with the suitcase?"

The shoemaker gave him a wink.

"You're not going to get cute with me, are you? I suppose I don't read the papers, do I? . . . Well, what were the papers going on about at the beginning? Didn't people come asking me whether I'd seen Frans go out with a suitcase, or his wife, or anyone else?"

"You saw the man in the photo go out with a suitcase?"

"Not that day. Anyhow, not that I noticed. I'm thinking of the other times."

"Did he come here often?"

"Yes, often."

"Once a week, for example? Or once a fortnight?"

"Maybe. I don't want to make anything up, because I know what a rough time the lawyers'll give me if this ever comes up in court. He used to come here often, and that's all I'm saying."

"In the morning? Afternoon?"

"My answer to that is: afternoon. Do you know why? . . . Because I can remember seeing him when the lights were on, so it must have been afternoon. He always had a small suitcase with him."

"Brown?"

"Probably. Aren't most suitcases brown? He would sit down in a corner of the shop, waiting for the work to be finished, and he'd leave again with the suitcase."

"Did that take long?"

"I don't know. More than an hour at least. Sometimes it seemed to me that he stayed the whole afternoon."

"Did he always come on the same day?"

"I can't tell you that either."

"Think before you answer. Did you ever see this man in the workshop at the same time as Madame Steuvels?"

"At the same time as Fernande? . . . Wait. I can't call it to mind. . . . Once, at least, the two men went out together, and Frans closed his shop."

"Recently?"

"I'll have to think. When are we going to have that drink?"

Maigret had no alternative but to follow him to the Grand Turenne, where the shoemaker assumed a triumphant manner.

"Two old brandies. On the chief inspector."

He drank three, one after another, and was trying to start the business of the clown all over again by the time

Maigret managed to get rid of him. When he passed the bookbinder's, Fernande was watching him through the glass door with an air of reproach.

But he had to keep on with his job to the end. He entered the lodge, where the concierge was busy peeling potatoes.

"Well, well. So you're back!" she observed tartly, offended at having been neglected for so long.

"Do you know this man?"

She went to fetch her glasses from a drawer.

"I don't know his name—if that's what you want—but I've seen him before. Didn't the shoemaker give you the information?"

She was put out because other people had been questioned first.

"Have you seen him often?"

"I've seen him—that's all I know."

"Was he a client of the bookbinder?"

"I suppose so, seeing he came to his shop."

"He didn't come for other reasons?"

"I think he occasionally had dinner with them. But I pay so little attention to my tenants!"

The stationer across the street, the cardboard manufacturer, the umbrella woman—in short, the routine: always the same questions, the same gestures, the picture, which people examined gravely. Some hesitated. Others had seen the man without remembering where or in what circumstances.

As he was leaving the neighborhood, Maigret had an impulse to push open the door of the Tabac des Vosges one last time.

"Have you ever seen this face before?"

The bartender did not hesitate.

"The man with the suitcase," he said.

"Explain."

"I don't know what he sells, but he must be a door-to-door salesman. He used to come in quite often, always a little while after lunch. He'd drink strawberry syrup with Vichy water. He explained to me that he had a stomach ulcer."

"Would he stay long?"

"Sometimes a quarter of an hour, sometimes longer. He always sat there, near the door."

From where he could keep an eye on the corner of Rue de Turenne!

"He must have been waiting till it was time for an appointment with a customer. Once, not so long ago, he stayed almost an hour, and finally asked for a telephone token."

"You don't know who he called?"

"No. When he came back, he left right away."

"In which direction?"

"I wasn't paying attention."

Since a reporter was coming in, the bartender asked Maigret in an undertone:

"Is it all right to talk about it?"

Maigret shrugged. There was no point in making mysteries, now that the shoemaker was in the know.

"If you want to."

When he entered Lucas's office, the inspector was coping with two telephones, and Maigret had to wait quite a while.

"I'm still hunting for the countess," Lucas said, mopping his forehead. "The people at the Wagons-Lits Company, who know her quite well, haven't seen her on any of their lines for several months. I've called most of the big hotels in Cannes, Nice, Antibes, and Villefranche. Nothing. I've also talked to the casinos; she hasn't set foot in any lately. Lapointe, because he speaks English, is telephoning Scotland Yard right now, and someone is taking care of the Italians."

Before going in to see Judge Dossin, Maigret went upstairs to have a word with Moers and return the useless photographs.

"No results?" asked poor Moers.

"One out of three. That's not bad. Now we only have to round up the other two. But it's possible they've never been through here."

At noon, there was still no sign of Countess Panetti, and two Italian reporters, who had been tipped off, were waiting, greatly excited, outside Maigret's office.

Maigret's Sunday

Madame Maigret had been rather surprised when, on Saturday, about three o'clock, her husband telephoned to find out whether dinner was cooking.

"Not yet. Why? . . . Yes, of course I'd like to. If you're sure you'll be free. Quite sure? . . . All right. I'll get dressed. . . . I'll be there. . . . Near the clock, yes. . . . No, no choucroute for me, but I'd love a *potée lorraine.* . . . What? You're not joking, are you? . . . Are you serious, Maigret? Anywhere I like? . . . That's too good to be true, and I feel sure you're going to call me back in an hour to tell me you won't be home to dinner or till morning. . . . Oh, well! I'll get ready anyway."

So, instead of smelling of cooking that Saturday, the apartment on Boulevard Richard-Lenoir smelled of bath salts and the flowery perfume Madame Maigret kept for special occasions.

Maigret was at the meeting place almost on time—

within five minutes. It was the Alsatian restaurant on Rue d'Enghien where they sometimes had dinner. Relaxed, with the air of thinking about the same things as other men, he ate choucroute prepared just the way he liked it.

"Have you decided on the movie?"

Because—and this had made Madame Maigret incredulous during the telephone call—he had invited her to spend the evening at any movie theater she chose.

They went to the Paramount on Boulevard des Italiens, and the chief inspector stood in line for the tickets without grumbling, merely emptying his pipe in an enormous spittoon in passing.

They heard electronic organ music and saw the orchestra emerge from the bowels of the earth on a platform while a curtain transformed itself into a sort of synthetic sunset. It was not until after the cartoons that Madame Maigret understood. A preview of the next movie had been shown, then some short reels advertising some kind of candy and furniture on the installment plan.

REQUEST FROM POLICE JUDICIAIRE:

It was the first time she had seen such a notice on the screen. Immediately after that, a rogues' gallery photograph was projected, first full face, then in profile: the picture of Alfred Moss, whose successive aliases were listed.

ANYBODY WHO SAW THIS MAN
IN THE LAST TWO MONTHS
IS REQUESTED TO TELEPHONE
IMMEDIATELY

113

"So that was it?" she said as they started to walk part of the way home in order to get some fresh air.

"That wasn't the only reason. . . . And by the way, the idea wasn't mine. It was suggested to the director ages ago, but there's never been an opportunity to try it out until now. Moers noticed that photographs published in the papers are always more or less distorted because of the halftone screen and the inking. Film projection, on the other hand, by enlarging the smallest characteristics, makes a more striking impression."

"Well anyway, whether that was the reason or not, it turned out nicely for me. How long is it since we did this?"

"Three weeks," he said in all sincerity.

"Exactly two and a half months!"

They pretended to squabble, for fun.

Next morning, because of the sun, which was again brilliant and springlike, Maigret sang in the bathtub. He walked all the way to the PJ, through almost deserted streets. It was always a pleasure to find the wide corridors of headquarters with doors standing open on vacant offices.

Lucas had only just arrived. Torrence was there too, as was Janvier. It wasn't long before Lapointe appeared. But because it was Sunday, they seemed to be working like amateurs. Perhaps it was also because it was Sunday that they left communicating doors open. From time to time, by way of music, they heard the bells of the local churches.

Lapointe was the only one who had brought in any new information. The previous night, before leaving, Maigret had asked him:

"By the way, where does that young reporter live who's flirting with your sister?"

114

"He's not flirting with her anymore. . . . You mean Antoine Bizard."

"They've broken up?"

"I don't know. Maybe he's afraid of me."

"I'd like his address."

"I don't know it, but I know where he eats most of his meals. I doubt that my sister knows any more. I'll ask at the paper."

Now, when he arrived, he handed a slip to Maigret. On it was the address in question: Rue Bergère, in the same apartment house as Philippe Liotard.

"That's fine, son. Thanks," the chief inspector said simply, without adding any comment.

If it had been a little warmer, he would have taken off his coat, just for the sake of being in his shirtsleeves, like people who putter around all day on Sunday, because puttering around was just what he felt like doing. All his pipes were lined up on his desk as he took out of his pocket his fat black notebook, which he always stuffed full of notes but almost never consulted.

Two or three times he threw into the wastebasket big sheets of paper, ruled into columns, on which he had scribbled, then changed his mind.

Finally, the work took a turn for the better.

Thursday, February 15. Countess Panetti, accompanied by her maid, Gloria Lotti, leaves the Claridge in the chocolate-colored Chrysler of her son-in-law, Krynker.

The date had been confirmed by the bell captain on the day shift. As for the car, the information had been furnished by one of the bellboys, who also reported the time of departure as seven o'clock at night. He had added that the old lady seemed worried and that her son-in-

115

law was hurrying her, as if they were about to miss a train or an important appointment.

Still no trace of the countess. He went into Lucas's office to make sure. The inspector was still receiving reports from all over the place.

The Italian reporters had gotten only a few scraps of information from the police the night before, but had furnished a few themselves. They did in fact know Countess Panetti. The marriage of her only daughter, Bella, had caused a big stir in Italy. Not able to get her mother's consent, the girl had run away from home to get married, in Monte Carlo.

That was five years ago, and since then the two families had never met.

If Krynker was in Paris, said one of the Italians, it was probably to attempt another reconciliation.

Friday, February 16. Gloria Lotti, wearing the countess's white hat, goes to Concarneau. There she sends a telegram to Fernande Steuvels and returns the same night without having met anyone.

In the margin Maigret had amused himself by drawing a woman's hat with a tiny veil.

Saturday, February 17. At noon Fernande leaves Rue de Turenne for Concarneau. Her husband does not accompany her to the station. About 4:00 a client comes to pick up some work he has commissioned. He finds Frans Steuvels in his workshop, where nothing seems out of the ordinary. Asked about the suitcase, he doesn't remember having seen it.

A few minutes past 8:00, three persons, among them Alfred Moss and probably the man who later registered on Rue Lepic under the name Levine, are taken by taxi

116

from the Gare Saint-Lazare to the corner of Turenne and Francs-Bourgeois.

The concierge hears knocking at Steuvels' door just before 9:00. She thinks the three men entered.

In the margin, in red pencil, he wrote: "Is the third character Krynker?"

Sunday, February 18. The furnace, not in use for the last few days, was going all night. Frans Steuvels has to make at least five trips into the courtyard to carry ashes to the ash cans.

Mademoiselle Béguin, tenant on the fifth floor, was inconvenienced by the smoke, "which had a funny smell."

Monday, February 19. Furnace is still going. The bookbinder is at home alone all day.

Tuesday, February 20. PJ receives anonymous note about a man burned in the bookbinder's furnace. Fernande returns from Concarneau.

Wednesday, February 21. Lapointe visits Rue de Turenne. He sees suitcase with handle mended with string under table in the workshop. Leaves workshop about noon. Has lunch with his sister and talks to her about the case. Does Mademoiselle Lapointe meet her young man, Antoine Bizard, who lives in the same building as the briefless lawyer Liotard? Or does she telephone him?

In the afternoon, before five, the lawyer calls at Rue de Turenne under the pretext of ordering a bookplate.

When Lucas makes his search, at five o'clock, suitcase has disappeared.

Interrogation of Steuvels at PJ. Toward morning, he names Maître Liotard as his lawyer.

Maigret stood up for a little stroll and a glance at the notes the inspectors were making at the telephones. It wasn't time yet to have beer sent up, and he simply filled another pipe instead.

Thursday, February 22.

Friday, February 23.

Saturday . . .

A whole column of dates with nothing opposite them, except that the inquiry was dragging; the papers were agitating; Liotard, snapping like a stray dog, was attacking the police in general and Maigret in particular. The right-hand column remained empty until:

Sunday, March 10. A man named Levine rents a room at Hotel Beauséjour on Rue Lepic and moves in with a little boy of about two.

Gloria Lotti, who passes for a nursemaid, looks after the child, whom she takes out every morning to Place d'Anvers while Levine is asleep.

She does not stay all night at the hotel, which she leaves very late, when Levine comes home.

Monday, March 11. Ditto.

Tuesday, March 12. 9:30: Gloria and the child leave Beauséjour as usual. 10:15: Moss appears at the hotel and asks for Levine. Latter immediately packs and takes his luggage down while Moss remains alone in the room.

10:55: Gloria sees Levine and instantly leaves the child, who remains in charge of Mme Maigret.

A little after 11:00: Gloria enters Beauséjour with Levine. They join Moss. All three argue for more than an hour. Moss leaves first.

About 1:00: Gloria and Levine leave hotel. Gloria gets into a taxi alone, goes back to Place d'Anvers, and picks up the child.

She takes the taxi as far as Porte de Neuilly, then says she wants to go to Gare Saint-Lazare and suddenly stops in Place Saint-Augustin, where she gets into another taxi. She leaves this one, still with the little boy, at the corner of Rue Montmartre and the Grands Boulevards.

The page was becoming ornamental, for Maigret was decorating it with drawings like a child's.

On another sheet he noted the dates on which they had lost track of the various characters:

Countess Panetti: Thursday evening, February 15

The garage attendant at the Claridge had been the last to see her, when she had stepped into her son-in-law's chocolate-colored Chrysler.

Krynker: ?

Maigret hesitated to write down the date Saturday, February 17, because they had no proof at all that he was the third person dropped by the taxi at the corner of Rue de Turenne.

If that was not he, his tracks disappeared simultaneously with the countess's.

Alfred Moss: Tuesday, March 12

He had been the first to leave the Hotel Beauséjour, about noon.

Levine: Tuesday, March 12

He left half an hour after the preceding character, and after seeing Gloria into a taxi.

Gloria and the child: Same date

They disappeared two hours later, in the crowd at the Carrefour Montmartre.

Today was Sunday, March 17. Since the twelfth, there had been nothing new to report—except for the investigation.

No; there was one date to note, which he added to the column:

Friday, March 15: Somebody in Métro tries(?) to pour poison into the dinner prepared for Frans Steuvels.

But that was still in doubt. The experts had found no trace of poison. In the state of nerves Fernande had been in recently, she might well have mistaken a passenger's clumsiness for a deliberate action.

At least it wasn't Moss, popping up again, because she would have recognized him.

Levine?

Maybe it was a message, not poison, that someone had tried to slip into the casserole.

Maigret, with a sunbeam catching him in the face, screwed up his eyes, and made a few more little drawings. Then he went to look at a string of barges going past on the Seine and at Pont Saint-Michel, filled with families in their Sunday clothes.

Madame Maigret had probably gone back to bed, as she sometimes did on Sundays, simply to make it seem more like Sunday, though she was incapable of going back to sleep.

"Janvier! What about ordering some beer?"

Janvier called the Brasserie Dauphine, and the proprietor asked, as a matter of course:

"And some sandwiches?"

Through a quiet telephone call, Maigret discovered that Judge Dossin, punctilious, was also in his office. He, no doubt, like the chief inspector, was hoping to sort things out in peace.

"Still no news of the car?"

It was amusing to think that on this beautiful Sunday, which smelled of spring, in the villages, where people were coming out of Mass and out of little cafés, hard-working policemen were keeping an eye on the cars, looking for the chocolate Chrysler.

"May I look, Chief?" asked Lucas, who had come to stretch his legs in Maigret's office between telephone calls.

He examined the chief inspector's work carefully. Then he shook his head.

"Why didn't you ask me? I've drawn the same diagram, in more detail."

"But without the little drawings," Maigret teased. "What's the leading item in the phone calls? Cars? Moss?"

"Cars, for the moment. Lots of chocolate cars. Unfortunately, when I pin them down, they're no longer exactly chocolate-colored, but reddish brown, or else they're Citroëns or Peugeots. We check anyhow. The

121

suburbs are beginning to phone in now, and the radius is expanding to about sixty miles from Paris."

In a little while, thanks to the radio, all France would be in on it. There was nothing to do but wait, and that wasn't so disagreeable. A man from the Brasserie brought a huge tray filled with glasses of beer and piles of sandwiches, and there was every chance that he would make more trips before the day was out.

The inspectors were soon eating and drinking, and they had just opened the windows, for the sun was warm, when they saw Moers come in, blinking his eyes as though he were emerging from a dark place.

They hadn't known he was in the building, where, theoretically, he had no business. Yet here he was, coming from upstairs, where he must be the only person in the laboratories.

"I'm sorry to bother you."

"A glass of beer? There's one left."

"No, thanks. As I was falling asleep last night, an idea kept bothering me. We were so sure that the blue suit unquestionably belonged to Steuvels that we examined it only for bloodstains. Since the suit's still here, I came in this morning to do an analysis of the dust."

This was, in fact, usually a routine procedure. Moers had sealed each piece of clothing in a strong paper bag and then had given the bag a good beating, in order to extract every trace of dust from the cloth.

"Find anything?"

"Sawdust, very fine, in remarkable quantities. It's really more like wood powder."

"The kind you might get in a sawmill?"

"No. That kind of sawdust would be less fine, less pervasive. Powder is produced by fine handwork."

"Cabinetwork, for instance?"

"Possibly. I'm not sure. It's even finer than that, in my opinion. But before I commit myself, I'd like to have a word with the head lab man tomorrow."

Without waiting to hear all this, Janvier had picked up a volume of the directory and was studying all the addresses on Rue de Turenne.

This yielded a list of various trades, some of them surprising, but by some chance nearly all connected with metal or cardboard.

"I thought I'd just mention it to you. I don't know whether it will help."

Neither did Maigret. In an investigation like this, they never knew what might help. At all events, the find tended to support the testimony of Frans Steuvels, who had always denied being the owner of the blue suit.

But then, why did he own a blue overcoat? A poor choice to go with a brown suit.

Telephones still rang. Sometimes six would be in use at the same time, and the switchboard operator was going out of his mind, because there were not enough people to take all the calls.

"What is it?"

"Lagny."

Maigret had been there once. It is a little town on the edge of the Marne, with a lot of men fishing and shiny canoes. He couldn't remember the case he had been on, but it was in summer, and he had drunk a light white wine, the memory of which was still with him.

Lucas was taking notes, indicating to the chief inspector that this seemed serious.

"Maybe we've got hold of something." He sighed as he hung up. "That was the Lagny police. For about a month, they've been quite excited down there about a car that fell in the river."

"It fell into the Marne a month ago?"

"As far as I could make out, yes. The man on the phone was so anxious to explain and go into detail that I couldn't make head or tail of it after a while. Besides, he kept dropping names I didn't know, as you might say Jesus Christ or Pasteur, and coming back over and over again to Old Mother Hébart or Hobart, who gets drunk every night but who is apparently incapable of making anything up. . . . To cut it short, about a month ago—"

"Did he tell you the exact date?"

"February 15."

Maigret, very pleased to find a use for it, consulted the list he had just drawn up.

Thursday, February 15. Countess Panetti, accompanied by her maid, Gloria Lotti, leaves the Claridge in the chocolate-colored Chrysler of her son-in-law, Krynker.

"I thought of that. This looks serious. You'll see. . . . So this old woman, who lives in an isolated house at the edge of the river—she rents canoes to fishermen in summer—went to the local bistro for a drink, as she does every evening. When she was going home, she claims, she heard a great crash. She's sure it was a car falling into the Marne.

"The river was in flood at the time. A minor road leading from the main highway ends at the water's edge, and the mud must have made it slippery."

"Did she report it to the police right away?"

"She talked about it in the bistro next day, but it took some time to get around. It finally reached the ears of a policeman, who questioned her.

"He went for a look, but the banks were partly submerged, and the current was so strong that navigation had to be suspended for a couple of weeks. Apparently the level is only now getting back to normal.

"I think the truth is they didn't take the matter seriously.

"Yesterday, after receiving our alert about the chocolate-colored car, they had a phone call from someone who lives at the corner of the highway and the minor road. He claims that last month he saw, in the darkness, a car that color turning in front of his house.

"He's a gas-station proprietor, who was filling up a customer's car, which explains why he was outside at that time."

"What time?"

"Just after nine o'clock."

It doesn't take two hours to get from the Champs-Elysées to Lagny, but of course there was nothing to prevent Krynker from making a detour.

"And so?"

"The police there asked the Highway Department for a crane."

"Yesterday?"

"Yesterday afternoon. There was a crowd watching it work. Anyhow, in the evening they caught something, but the darkness kept them from going on. They even told me the name of the hole, because the river holes are well known to fishermen and local people. There's one that's thirty feet deep."

"Have they fished the car out yet?"

"This morning. It really is a Chrysler, chocolate-colored, with an Alpes-Maritimes registration number.

"That's not all. There's a body inside."

"Male?"

"Female. It's terribly decomposed. Most of the clothing's been torn off by the current. . . . The body is still on the bank, under a tarpaulin, and they want to know what they're to do with it. I said I'd call back."

Moers had left a few minutes too soon. He was the man who would have been invaluable to the chief inspector, but there wasn't much chance of finding him at home yet.

"Would you call Dr. Paul?"

The doctor answered in person.

"You're not busy? No plans for the day? . . . Would it be too inconvenient if I came over and picked you up to take you to Lagny? . . . With your bag, yes. . . . No. It probably won't be a pretty sight. An old woman who's spent a month in the Marne."

Maigret looked around and saw Lapointe glancing away and blushing. The young man was obviously burning with the desire to accompany his chief.

"You haven't a date this afternoon?"

"Oh, no, sir."

"Can you drive?"

"I've had my license for two years."

"Go and get the blue Peugeot and wait for me downstairs. Check the gas."

To Janvier, who looked disappointed, he said:

"You take another car and drive there slowly, questioning garagemen, wine merchants, anyone you like. It's possible that somebody else may have noticed the chocolate car. I'll see you in Lagny."

He drank the extra glass of beer. Shortly after, Dr. Paul cheerfully settled himself in the car Lapointe was proudly driving.

"Shall I take the shortest way?"

"Preferably, young man."

It was one of the first fine Sundays, and there were a

lot of cars on the road, crammed with whole families and their picnic baskets.

Dr. Paul told stories of autopsies, which, from his lips, were as funny as jokes about fools.

At Lagny, they had to ask directions, go through the little town, and make some long detours before arriving at a bend in the river where a crane was surrounded by at least a hundred people. The police were having as much trouble as they did on fair day. An officer was on the scene, and he seemed relieved to see the chief inspector.

The chocolate car, covered with mud, grass, and un-identifiable flotsam, was there, upside down on the bank, with water still trickling from its cracks. Its body was bent out of shape, one of the windows was broken, both headlights were shattered; but by an extraordinary chance one door was still working, and through this they had extricated the body.

It formed a little heap under the tarpaulin, which no sightseer could approach without his stomach turning.

"I'll leave you to it, Doctor."

"Here?"

Dr. Paul would have been willing to do it. With his eternal cigarette in his mouth, he had been known to carry out autopsies in the most unlikely places, and even to stop and take off his rubber gloves in order to eat a snack.

"Can we take the body to the police station?" he asked the police officer.

"My men will see to it. Stand back, everybody. . . . And the children! Who's letting children come so close?"

Maigret was examining the car when an old woman plucked his sleeve and said proudly:

"It was me who found it."

"Are you Widow Hébart?"

"Hubart, sir. That's my house you can see behind the ash trees."

"Tell me what you saw."

"I didn't see anything, but I heard. I was coming back along the towpath. That's the path we're on."

"Had you had a lot to drink?"

"Only two or three."

"Where were you?"

"Fifteen feet from here, farther on, nearer my house. I heard a car coming in from the highway, and I said to myself it must be poachers again. Because it was too cold for lovers, and it was raining too. All I saw, when I turned around, was the headlights. . . .

"I didn't know this was going to be important someday, did I? I kept on walking, but I thought the car stopped."

"Because you couldn't hear the motor anymore?"

"Yes."

"You had your back to the road?"

"Yes . . . Then I heard the motor again, and I thought the car was turning around. Not at all! Right then there was a big plouf, and when I looked around, the car was gone."

"You didn't hear any shouting?"

"No."

"You didn't go back?"

"Why should I? What could I do all by myself? . . . It upset me. I thought the poor people were drowned, so I hurried home to get a drink, to revive me."

"You didn't stay by the water?"

"No, sir."

"You didn't hear anything after the plouf?"

"I thought I heard something, footsteps maybe, but

128

then I decided it must be a rabbit, frightened by the noise."

"Is that all?"

"Don't you think it's enough? If they'd listened to me, instead of treating me like a crazy old fool, the lady would have been out of the water long ago. Have you seen her?"

Not without a grimace of disgust, Maigret imagined this old woman contemplating the other, decomposed, old woman.

Did the Widow Hubart realize that it was a miracle she was still alive, that if her curiosity had impelled her to turn back on that notable evening, she would probably have followed the other woman into the Marne?

"Won't the reporters be coming?"

That's what she was waiting for: to have her picture in the papers.

Lapointe, covered with mud, was climbing out of the Chrysler, which he had examined.

"I didn't find a thing," he said. "The tools are in their place in the trunk, with the spare tire. There's no luggage, no handbag. There was only a woman's shoe, caught in the back of the seat, and in the glove compartment this pair of gloves and this flashlight."

The pigskin gloves were men's, so far as one could tell.

"Go over to the railway station. Someone must have taken the train that night. Unless there are taxis in town. Meet me at the police station."

He preferred to wait in the courtyard, smoking his pipe, until Dr. Paul, installed in the garage, had finished his job.

The Toy Family

"Are you disappointed, Monsieur Maigret?"

Young Lapointe was longing to say "Chief," like Lucas, Torrence, and most of the rest of the Crime Squad, but he felt too much of a newcomer for that. It seemed to him that this was a privilege he would have to earn, like winning one's spurs.

They had just driven Dr. Paul home and were on their way back to the Quai des Orfèvres, in a Paris that seemed more luminous after the hours they'd spent floundering in the dismal atmosphere of Lagny. From Pont Saint-Michel, Maigret could see the light in his office.

"I'm not disappointed. I wasn't expecting the railway employees to remember passengers whose tickets they punched a month ago."

"I was wondering what you had in mind."

He replied, quite naturally:

"The suitcase."

"I swear it was in the workshop when I went to the bookbinder's."

"I don't doubt it."

"And I'm positive it wasn't the one that Lucas found that afternoon in the basement."

"I don't doubt that either. Leave the car in the yard and come up."

From the animation of the few men on duty there, it was clear that something had happened, and Lucas, hearing Maigret come in, hastily opened his office door.

"Some information on Moss, Chief. . . . A young woman and her father were here earlier. They wanted to speak to you personally, but after waiting almost two hours, they decided to give me the message.

"She's a pretty girl of sixteen or seventeen, plump and rosy, who looks you frankly in the eye. The father's a sculptor, who, if I got it right, once won the Prix de Rome. There's another girl, at home, a little older, and a mother. They live on Boulevard Pasteur, where they manufacture toys.

"If I'm not mistaken, the girl came along to keep her father from stopping for a drink, which seems to be his besetting sin. He wears a big black hat and a flowing scarf.

"Moss, going by the name Peeters, has been living in their house for the last few months."

"Is he still there?"

"If he were, I would have sent some of the men over to arrest him, or I'd have gone myself. He left them on March 12."

In other words, the day Levine, Gloria, and the child disappeared from circulation after the event in the Place d'Anvers park.

"He didn't tell them he was leaving. He went out in

the morning as usual, and hasn't set foot in the apartment since. I thought you'd prefer to interrogate them yourself. . . . Oh, and something else: Philippe Liotard has telephoned twice."

"What does *he* want?"

"To speak to you. He asked if you'd call him at the Chope du Nègre if you came in before eleven."

Maigret knew that café on Boulevard Bonne-Nouvelle.

"Get me the Chope."

It was the cashier who answered. She had the lawyer paged.

"Is that you, Chief Inspector? I suppose you're swamped with work. . . . Have you found him?"

"Who?"

"Moss. I went to the movies this afternoon, and I caught on. Don't you think an off-the-record conversation might be useful to us both?"

A little earlier, in the car, Maigret had been thinking about the suitcase. Now, while Liotard was talking to him, Lapointe came into the office, and, by chance, his thought expanded.

"Are you with friends?" the chief inspector asked Liotard.

"That doesn't matter. When you get here, I'll leave them."

"Your lady friend?"

"Yes."

"No one else?"

"Somebody you're not very fond of—why, I don't know—and who's very distressed about it."

Alfonsi. The foursome again, the two men and their girls.

"Would you have the patience to wait for me if I'm late?"

"I'll wait as long as you like. It's Sunday."

"Tell Alfonsi I'd like to see him too."

"He'll be charmed."

He went and closed the two doors to his office, telling Lapointe, who'd been about to go out, to stay.

"Come here. Sit down. . . . You want to get ahead in the police, don't you?"

"More than anything."

"You made the stupid mistake of talking too much the other day, and this has had consequences you don't even suspect yet."

"I'm really sorry. I had complete confidence in my sister."

"Do you want to try something difficult? Wait! Don't be in too much of a hurry to answer. It's not a matter of a glorious stunt that will get your name in the papers. Quite the contrary. If you succeed, nobody but the two of us will ever know about it. If you fail, I'll be obliged to disclaim all responsibility and maintain that you were acting on your own."

"I understand."

"You don't understand at all, but that doesn't matter. If I were to take the job on myself and fail, the whole of the police force would be involved. You're new enough to get away with it."

Lapointe could not hide his impatience.

"Maître Liotard and Alfonsi are at the Chope du Nègre. They're waiting for me."

"Are you going to join them?"

"Not right away. First, I want to make a call on Boulevard Pasteur, but I'm sure they won't budge from the café before I get there. I'll join them in an hour at the earliest. It's nine o'clock. . . . You know where the lawyer lives, on Rue Bergère? It's the fourth floor, left. Since a number of young ladies live in that building, the concierge probably doesn't pay too much attention to who comes and goes."

"You want me to . . ."

"Yes. You've been taught how to open a door. It won't matter if you leave marks. Quite the contrary. No sense in going through drawers and papers. You're to make sure of just one thing: that the suitcase isn't there."

"I never thought of that."

"Well, it's possible, and even probable, that it isn't there, because Liotard is a cautious fellow. That's why you mustn't waste any time. From Rue Bergère you're to go straight over to Rue de Douai, where Alfonsi has room 33 in the Hotel du Massif Central."

"I know."

"Do the same thing there. The suitcase. Nothing else. Call me as soon as you're through."

"Can I leave now?"

"Go out into the corridor first. I'm going to lock my door; you try to open it. Ask Lucas for the tools."

Lapointe didn't do too badly, and a few minutes later he was hurrying out, utterly happy.

Maigret went next door.

"Are you free, Janvier?"

The telephones were still ringing, but, because of the time of night, with less frequency.

"I was giving Lucas a hand, but . . ."

They went downstairs together, and Janvier took the wheel of the little police car. A quarter of an hour later, they reached the quietest, least brightly lighted stretch of Boulevard Pasteur, which, in the peace of a beautiful

Sunday evening, looked like the main avenue of some small town.

"Come up with me."

They asked for the sculptor, whose name was Grossot, and were directed to the seventh floor. The building, old but well kept, was probably inhabited mostly by minor government employees. When they knocked at the door of the apartment, the sounds of an argument suddenly ceased. A young girl with full cheeks opened the door and stepped back.

"Was it you who came to my office earlier?"

"That was my sister. Chief Inspector Maigret? Come in. Pay no attention to the mess. We're just finishing dinner."

She led them into a huge studio, with a sloping ceiling, partly glass, beyond which stars could be seen. The remains of some cold cuts and an open liter of wine were on a long pine table. Another girl, who looked like the twin of the one who had opened the door, was tidying her hair with furtive movements. A man in a velvet jacket approached the visitors with exaggerated solemnity.

"Welcome to my modest abode, Monsieur Maigret. I hope you will do me the honor of having a drink with me."

Since leaving the PJ, the old sculptor must have managed to get something to drink besides table wine, because his speech was impaired, his gait unsteady.

"Don't pay any attention," interposed one of the girls. "He's got himself in that state again."

She said this without rancor, and the look she gave her father was affectionate, almost maternal.

In the darkest corners of the room, pieces of sculpture could be vaguely sensed, and it was clear that they had been there for a long time.

More recent, part of their present life, were the carved wooden toys lying around on the furniture and filling the room with a good smell of fresh wood.

"When art no longer offers a living to a man and his family," Grossot was declaiming, "there's nothing to be ashamed of—is there?—in looking to commerce for one's daily bread."

Madame Grossot appeared; she must have gone to tidy up when she heard the bell. She was a thin woman, sad, with constantly watchful eyes, who must always be foreseeing misfortune.

"Won't you give the chief inspector and this gentleman a chair, Hélène?"

"The chief inspector knows perfectly well that he can make himself at home here, Mother. Don't you, Monsieur Maigret?"

"Didn't you offer him anything?"

"Would you like a glass of wine? There's nothing else in the house, on account of Papa."

She seemed to be the one who controlled the family; at all events, the one who was taking control of the conversation.

"We went to the movies yesterday, in this neighborhood, and we recognized the man you're looking for. He was using the name Peeters, not Moss. . . . The reason we didn't come to see you earlier was that Papa hesitated to turn him in. He protested that Peeters has been our guest and eaten at our table several times."

"Has he been living here long?"

"About a year. Our apartment occupies the whole floor. My parents have lived here more than thirty years, and I was born here, as was my sister. There are three rooms besides the studio and the kitchen. Last year, the toys didn't bring in much, and we decided to take a boarder. We put an advertisement in the paper.

"That's how we got to know Monsieur Peeters."

"What did he say his profession was?"

"He told us that he represented a big English mill and that he had his own customers, so there was no need for him to go out much. Sometimes he'd spend the whole day here; he'd come and give us a hand, in his shirtsleeves. We all work on the toys, for which my father makes the models. Last Christmas, we got an order from Printemps, and we worked night and day."

Grossot was eying the half-empty wine bottle so pathetically that Maigret said to him:

"Oh, well, pour me half a glass, just for the sake of having a drink with you."

He received in return a look of gratitude. The girl continued talking, but without taking her eyes off her father, to be sure he didn't help himself too freely:

"He usually went out late in the afternoon, and he sometimes came home quite late. Occasionally, he'd take his sample case with him."

"Did he leave his luggage here?"

"He left his big trunk."

"Not his suitcase?"

"No. Olga, did he have his suitcase when he left?"

"No. He didn't bring it back last time he took it with him."

"What kind of man was he?"

"He was quiet, gentle, rather sad. Sometimes he stayed shut up in his room for hours at a time. And we'd finally go and ask if he was ill. Other times he'd have breakfast with us and help us all day.

"Occasionally he would disappear for several days, but he'd tell us beforehand not to worry about him."

"What did you call him?"

"Monsieur Jean. He called us by our first names, except my mother, of course. He sometimes brought us candy or little presents."

"Never expensive presents?"

"We wouldn't have accepted them."

"He never had visitors?"

"Nobody ever came. He never got any mail either. I was surprised that a businessman wouldn't receive any letters, but he explained to me that he had a partner in town, with an office, and his correspondence was addressed there."

"Did he ever seem odd to you?"

At this she glanced around and murmured, though without emphasis:

"Well, here, you know!"

"Your health, Monsieur Maigret! To your investigation! As you can see, I no longer count for anything, not only in the domain of art, but also in my own house. I don't protest. I say nothing. They're very nice, but for a man who—"

"Let the chief inspector talk, Papa."

"You see?"

"You don't know when your boarder went out with his suitcase for the last time?"

It was Olga, the older girl, who answered:

"The Saturday before . . ."

She debated whether she ought to continue.

"Before what?"

The younger girl reassumed control of the interview.

"Don't blush, Olga. We're always teasing my sister, because she had a crush on Monsieur Jean. He wasn't the right age for her and he wasn't handsome, but . . ."

"What about yourself?"

138

"Never mind that, Olga. . . . One Saturday, about six o'clock, he went out with his suitcase, which was surprising, because it was usually on Mondays that he took it with him."

"Monday afternoons?"

"Yes. We weren't expecting him back, thinking he was going away for the weekend somewhere, and we were making fun of Olga, who was moping."

"That's not true."

"We haven't the slightest idea what time he came home. Usually we'd hear him open the door. On Sunday morning, we thought his room was empty and we were just talking about him when he came out, looking ill, and asked my father if he would mind getting him a bottle of brandy. He said he'd caught cold. He stayed in bed part of the day. Olga, who takes care of his room, noticed that the suitcase wasn't there. She noticed something else—at least she claims she did."

"I'm sure of it."

"You may be right. You looked at him more closely than we did."

"I'm sure his suit wasn't the same one. It was a blue suit too, but not his, and when he had it on, I noticed that it was too big at the shoulder."

"He didn't say anything about it?"

"No. We didn't mention it either. After that, he complained that he was coming down with the flu, and he stayed here for a whole week without going out."

"Did he read the papers?"

"Morning and evening, just as we do."

"You didn't notice anything out of the ordinary?"

"No . . . Except that he'd go and shut himself up in his room the minute anybody knocked at the door."

"When did he start going out again?"

"About a week later. The last time he slept here was the night of March 11. That's easy to be sure of, because on the calendar in his room the leaves haven't been torn off since then."

"What ought we to do, Chief Inspector?" asked the mother anxiously.

"I don't know, madame."

"If the police are looking for him . . ."

"May we have a look at his room?"

It was at the end of a hall. Spacious, not luxurious, but clean, it contained old waxed furniture and reproductions of Michelangelo on the walls. An enormous black trunk of the most common kind was in the right-hand corner, tied with cord.

"Open it, Janvier."

"Shall I leave?" asked the girl.

He didn't see any necessity for that. Janvier had more trouble with the cord than with the lock, which was a common kind. A strong smell of mothballs pervaded the room, and suits, shoes, underwear began to pile up on the bed.

It might have been an actor's wardrobe, judging by the range of quality and origin in the clothing. A set of tails and a dinner jacket bore the label of a well-known London tailor, and another dress suit had been made in Milan.

There were also some white linen suits, the kind worn mainly in hot countries; some pretty loud outfits; and others that, on the contrary, might have belonged to a bank teller. For all of them, there were matching shoes, bought in Paris, Nice, Brussels, Rotterdam, or Berlin.

At the very bottom, separated from the rest by a sheet of brown paper, they unearthed a clown's costume, which the girl stared at in bewilderment.

"Was he an actor?"

"In his own way."

There was nothing else revealing in the room. The blue suit they had been talking about wasn't there. Peeters-Moss was wearing it when he left; perhaps he was still wearing it.

In the drawers, small objects: cigarette cases, a wallet, cuff links and studs, keys, a broken pipe, but not one document and no address book.

"Thank you, mademoiselle. It was very sensible of you to inform us, and I'm sure you won't regret it. Do you have a telephone?"

"We used to have one a few years ago, but . . ."

And in a low voice:

"Papa hasn't always been like this. That's why we can't hold it against him. He used not to drink at all. Then he met some old friends from the Beaux Arts who are in the same boat, and he got into the habit of going out with them to a little café in Saint-Germain. It didn't do them any good."

A bench in the studio held several precision tools for sawing, gluing, and planing the tiny pieces of wood from which they made miniature toys.

"Take some sawdust in a paper, Janvier."

This would please Moers. It was amusing to think that through his analysis alone they would inevitably have made their way finally to this apartment perched high in a building on Boulevard Pasteur. It would have taken weeks, possibly months, but they would have got here just the same.

It was ten o'clock. The wine bottle was empty, and Grossot proposed to accompany "these gentlemen" down to the street, which he was not permitted to do.

"I'll probably be back."

"And the other one?"

"I don't expect so. In any case, I don't think you have anything at all to fear from him."

"Where shall I drop you, Chief?" asked Janvier, taking the wheel of the car.

"Boulevard Bonne-Nouvelle. Not too near the Chope du Nègre. Wait for me."

It was one of those big cafés that serve sauerkraut and sausage, where on Saturday and Sunday evenings four half-starved musicians play on a stage. Maigret immediately spied the two couples, not far from the front window; noted that the two women had ordered green crème de menthe.

Alfonsi was the first to stand up, not completely sure of himself, like a man who expects a kick, while the lawyer, smiling and self-possessed, held out his well-kept hand.

"May I introduce our friends?"

He did so condescendingly.

"Would you like to sit down for a minute at this table or do you want to move to another one?"

"On condition that Alfonsi keeps the women company and waits for me, I'd rather hear what you have to say now."

A table near the cashier was vacant. The clientele was mainly made up of local shopkeepers treating their families to dinner in a restaurant, just as Maigret had done the night before. There were also some regular customers: bachelors or unhappily married men, playing cards or checkers.

"What will you have? . . . A beer? One beer and one brandy-and-water, waiter."

It would probably not be long before Liotard was frequenting bars near the Opéra and the Champs-Élysées,

142

but for the present he felt more at home in this neighborhood, where he could stare at people with an air of great superiority.

"Has your announcement brought any results?"

"Was it to question me, Maître Liotard, that you invited me to come and see you?"

"Maybe it was to make peace. What would you say to that? . . . Perhaps I was a bit short with you. Don't forget that we're on opposite sides of the fence. Your job is to bear down on my client; mine is to save him."

"Even by becoming his accomplice?"

The shot went home. The young lawyer with the long, pinched nostrils blinked two or three times.

"I don't know what you mean. But if that's the way you want it, I'll come straight to the point. As luck has it, Chief Inspector, you're in a position to do me a lot of harm: to delay, if not interrupt, a career that everyone agrees will be brilliant."

"I don't doubt it."

"Thank you. The Bar Association is pretty strict about certain rules, and I admit that in my hurry to get ahead I haven't always stuck to them."

Maigret was drinking his beer with the most innocent air in the world, watching the cashier. She could easily have mistaken him for the hatmaker from the shop around the corner.

"I'm waiting, Maître Liotard."

"I hoped you might help me, because you know very well what I'm referring to."

Maigret did not react.

"You know, Chief Inspector, I come from a poor family, very poor—"

"The counts Liotard?"

"I said very poor, not commoners. I had a hard time

143

paying my way through law school, and when I was a student I had to take all kinds of jobs. I even wore a uniform in a large movie theater."

"Congratulations."

"Even a month ago, I wasn't eating every day. I was waiting, like all my colleagues of my age, and some older ones too, for a case that would give me a chance to distinguish myself."

"You found it."

"I found it. That's what I'm getting at. On Friday, in Monsieur Dossin's office, you uttered certain words that made me think you knew a great deal about this business and that you wouldn't hesitate to use it against me."

"Against you?"

"Against my client, if you prefer."

"I don't understand."

Of his own accord, Maigret ordered another beer, because he had rarely drunk any as good, especially in contrast to the sculptor's lukewarm wine. He was still watching the cashier, as if he was glad she looked so much like old-fashioned café cashiers, with her big bust pushed up by her corset, her black silk blouse ornamented with a cameo, her hair like a set piece in a hairdresser's window.

"You were saying?"

"All right, if that's the way you want it. You're determined to make me come clean, and you've got the whip hand. I made a professional error in soliciting Steuvels to become my client."

"Only one?"

"I happened to hear about the whole thing in a perfectly routine way, and I hope no one is going to have any trouble on my account. . . . I'm quite friendly with a certain Antoine Bizard; we live in the same building.

144

We've been through the mill together. We've been reduced to sharing a can of sardines or a Camembert.
. . . Recently Bizard got a steady job on a newspaper. He has a girlfriend—"

"The sister of one of my men."

"So you do know."

"I like hearing you tell it."

"Through his job on the paper—he's a legman—Bizard is in a position to hear about certain matters before they become public."

"Crimes, for instance."

"If you like. He's gotten into the habit of calling me."

"So you can go over and offer your services?"

"You're a cruel winner, Monsieur Maigret."

"Go on."

He was still looking at the cashier, but at the same time making sure that Alfonsi was keeping the two women occupied.

"I was informed that the police were interested in a bookbinder on Rue de Turenne."

"On February 21, early in the afternoon."

"That's right. I went over there, and I really did talk about a bookplate before bringing up a hotter matter."

"The furnace."

"That's all. I told Steuvels that if he was in any trouble I'd be glad to defend him. You know all that. . . . And it was not so much for my own sake that I instigated the conversation we've had tonight—which I trust will remain strictly between the two of us—as for my client's. Anything that would harm me at the moment would harm him by repercussion. . . . There it is, Monsieur Maigret. It's for you to decide. I may be suspended from the bar tomorrow morning. All you have to do is go and see the president and tell him what you know."

"Did you stay at the bookbinder's long?"

"Fifteen minutes at the most."

"Did you see his wife?"

"I think at one point she stuck her head out of the stairwell."

"Did Steuvels take you into his confidence?"

"No. I'll give you my word of honor on that."

"One more question, Liotard. How long has Alfonsi been working for you?"

"He's not working for me. He's running a private detective agency."

"Of which he's the only employee!"

"That's none of my business. To defend my client with any chance of success, I need certain information that it would be unbecoming for me to dig up for myself."

"Primarily, you needed to be kept up to date on what I know."

"That's fair enough, isn't it?"

The cashier picked up the telephone, which had just rung, and answered:

"Hold on a minute. I'll find out."

As she opened her mouth to give a name to a waiter, the chief inspector stood up.

"Is it for me?"

"What's your name?"

"Maigret."

"Do you want to take it in the booth?"

"Never mind. I'll be only a second."

It was the call he was expecting from Lapointe, whose voice was tense with excitement.

"Is that you, Chief Inspector? *I've got it!*"

"Where?"

"I didn't find anything at the lawyer's, where I nearly got caught by the concierge. I went over to Rue de Douai.

146

There were crowds of people going in and out there. It was easy. I had no trouble opening the door. The suitcase was under the bed. What shall I do with it?"

"Where are you?"

"At the cigar store on the corner of Douai."

"Take a taxi to the office. I'll meet you there."

"Yes, *Chief*. Are you pleased?"

Carried away by his enthusiasm and pride, he was venturing the word for the first time, though not with complete confidence.

"You've done a good job."

The lawyer was watching Maigret uneasily. The chief inspector sat down again on the banquette, gave a sigh of satisfaction, and signaled the waiter.

"Another beer. It might be a good idea to bring this gentleman a brandy."

"But . . ."

"Pipe down, boy."

This made the lawyer gasp with indignation.

"Look. It's not the Bar Association I'm going to report you to. It's the public prosecutor. Tomorrow morning I'll probably ask him for two arrest warrants, one in your name, one in that of your crony Alfonsi."

"Are you joking?"

"What are you likely to get for suppression of evidence in a murder case? I'll have to look it up. . . . I'll think it over. May I leave the check to you?"

Already on his feet, he added softly, confidentially, leaning over Philippe Liotard's shoulder:

"I've got the suitcase!"

The Dieppe Snapshot

Maigret had called the judge's office the first time at about half past nine and spoken to the clerk.

"Would you ask Monsieur Dossin if he can see me?"

"Here he is now."

"Something new?" the judge had asked. "I mean besides what's in the morning paper?"

The papers had reported the discovery of the chocolate-colored car and the body of the old woman at Lagny.

"I think so. May I come and tell you about it."

Since then, every time the chief inspector started for the door of his office, something had delayed him—a telephone call or the arrival of an inspector who had a report to make.

The judge had called back discreetly and asked Lucas:

"Is the chief inspector still there?"

"Yes. Shall I put him on?"

"No. I suppose he's busy. I'm sure he'll be up in a minute."

At quarter after ten, he made up his mind to get Maigret on the line.

"Sorry to bother you. You must be swamped. But I'm having Frans Steuvels brought in at eleven, and I don't want to begin the interrogation before seeing you."

"Would you mind if your interrogation turned into a confrontation?"

"Who with?"

"With his wife, probably. If I may, I'll get one of my men to bring her in, just on the chance."

"Do you want a formal confrontation?"

"That won't be necessary."

Dossin waited a good ten minutes more, pretending to study the dossier. At last there was a knock at the door. He almost made a rush for it as he saw Maigret silhouetted there, a suitcase in his hand.

"Are you going away?"

The chief inspector's smile enlightened him, and he murmured, not able to believe his eyes:

"The suitcase?"

"It's heavy, I can tell you."

"So we were right?"

He was relieved of a great weight. The systematic campaign of Philippe Liotard had shaken him. It was he, after all, who had taken the responsibility for keeping Steuvels in prison.

"Is he guilty?"

"Guilty enough to be put inside for several years."

Maigret had known the contents of the suitcase since the previous evening, but he made the inventory again, with all the pleasure of a child setting out his Christmas presents.

What made the reddish-brown suitcase with the handle mended with string so heavy were some pieces of metal, which looked like bookbinder's stamps but were actually the seals of various sovereign states.

Conspicuous among them were those of the United States and of all the South American republics.

There were also rubber stamps like those used in city halls and government offices, all arranged as carefully as a salesman's samples.

"Steuvels' work," explained Maigret. "His brother Alfred provided him with the models and the blank passports. As far as I can tell from these specimens, the passports weren't counterfeit, but were obtained by theft from consulates."

"Has he been in this business long?"

"I don't think so. Two years roughly, judging by the bank accounts. In fact, this morning I telephoned most of the banks in Paris, and that's partly what kept me from coming up to see you earlier."

"Steuvels has an account at the Société Générale on Rue Saint-Antoine, hasn't he?"

"He has another in an American bank on Place Vendôme, and another in a British bank on the boulevard. So far, we've found five accounts. They were opened two years ago, which corresponds with when his brother came back to Paris to live."

It was gray and raining. The weather was mild. Maigret sat by the window, smoking his pipe.

"You see, Judge, Alfred Moss doesn't fall into the category of professional criminals. Those men have one specialty, and most of the time they stick to it. I've never known a pickpocket to turn burglar or a burglar to pass bad checks or try the confidence game.

"Alfred Moss is a clown, first and foremost, and an acrobat.

"It was as a result of a fall that he got into this business. If I'm not greatly mistaken, he did his first job by chance, when, cashing in on his knowledge of languages, he was hired by a big London hotel as an interpreter. An opportunity arose to steal some jewelry, and he seized it.

"This was enough for him to live on for a time. Not for long, because he has one vice. I found this out this morning too, from his local bookie. He plays the horses.

"Like any amateur, he didn't stick to one type of theft; he wanted to try everything. The confidence game would follow passing bad checks.

"He did it all with unusual skill and luck. It's never been possible to prove anything against him.

"But he had his ups and downs.

"Finally, he wasn't as young as he used to be, and he was known to the police in most capitals and was black-listed by the big hotels where he regularly operated."

"That's when he remembered his brother?"

"Yes. Two years ago, the gold traffic, which was his major activity then, wasn't paying off anymore. On the other hand, fake passports, especially for America, were beginning to bring astronomical prices. He figured that a bookbinder, accustomed to reproducing coats of arms by means of stamps and blocks, would be able to do just as good a job with official seals."

"What amazes me is that Steuvels, who doesn't lack for anything, should have accepted . . . unless he leads a double life we haven't discovered."

"He doesn't lead any double life. Poverty—real poverty, of the kind he knew in his childhood and adolescence—produces two kinds of people: free spenders and

151

misers. It more often produces misers, and they're so afraid of seeing the bad days return that they're capable of anything at all to provide against that.

"I'd guess that's the case with Steuvels. The list of his bank accounts offers additional proof. I'm sure this wasn't just a way of hiding his nest egg, because it never occurred to him that he might be found out. Instead, he was suspicious of banks and of nationalization and devaluation, and that's why he used different banking houses."

"I thought he almost never went out without his wife."

"That's right. It was she who went out without him, and it took me some time to discover that. On Monday afternoons, she went to the Vert-Galant laundry barge to do her washing. Almost every Monday, Moss would arrive with his suitcase; when he was early, he'd wait at the Tabac des Vosges until his sister-in-law had left.

"The two brothers had the afternoon before them for their work. The tools and the compromising documents never remained at Rue de Turenne. Moss took them away with him.

"On some Mondays, Steuvels would have time to hurry to one of his banks and make a deposit."

"I don't see what part was played by the young woman with the child, or by Countess Panetti or—"

"I'm coming to that, Judge. I told you about the suit-case first because that's what bothered me more than anything right from the start. But ever since I learned of the existence of Moss, and suspected what he was up to, I've had another question on my mind.

"Why, on Tuesday, March 12, all of a sudden, when everything seemed quiet, was there that unusual flare-up, which ended in the group's dispersing?

"I mean the incident in the Place d'Anvers park, which my wife happened to witness.

"Only the night before, Moss was living peacefully in his furnished room on Boulevard Pasteur.

"Levine and the child were staying at the Hotel Beauséjour, where Gloria would pick up the child every morning to take him out.

"On that Tuesday, about ten in the morning, Moss entered the Hotel Beauséjour, where, probably as a precaution, he had never set foot.

"Immediately after, Levine packed, dashed over to Place d'Anvers, called Gloria, who deserted the child in order to follow him.

"By afternoon they'd all disappeared, leaving no trace.

"What happened on the morning of March 12?

"Moss couldn't have received a telephone call, because the house he lives in has no telephone.

"Neither I nor my men made any move at that time that might have alarmed the group, the existence of which we didn't even suspect.

"As for Frans Steuvels, he was in Santé.

"All the same, something did happen.

"And it was only last night, when I went home, that, through the wildest chance, I found the answer."

Dossin was so relieved to know that the man he had put in prison was not innocent that he was listening with a sort of fascinated smile, as he might have listened to a joke.

"My wife had been waiting for me all evening, and had spent the time catching up on a little job she takes care of now and again. This consists of keeping scrapbooks of newspaper clippings that mention me, and she does it more devotedly than ever since a former commissioner of police published his memoirs.

"When I make fun of this hobby, she says: 'Well, you might write yours someday, after you've retired and we're living in the country.'

"Anyway, when I got home last night, the scissors and paste were on the table. I happened to glance over my wife's shoulder, and in one of the clippings she was about to paste in, I saw a photograph I had completely forgotten.

"It had been taken three years ago by a local reporter in Normandy. We were spending a few days in Dieppe, and he'd caught us—my wife and me—on the steps of our pension.

"What amazed me was to see it on a page from a picture magazine.

"My wife said: 'Didn't you see it? It came out recently— a four-page article on the early days of your career and your methods.'

"There were some other photographs—one of me when I was a district secretary and had a drooping mustache.

" 'What's the date of it?' I asked her.

" 'Of the article? Last week. I haven't had time to show it to you. You've hardly been home lately.'

"In short, Judge, the article appeared in a Paris weekly that went on sale on the morning of Tuesday, March 12.

"I immediately sent someone over to see the people Moss was still living with on that date, and they confirmed that the younger of the girls had taken the magazine in with the milk, at about half past eight, and that Moss had glanced at it while he was having breakfast.

"From then on everything's straightforward. This even explains Gloria's long sessions on the park bench in Place d'Anvers.

"After their two murders and the arrest of Steuvels, the group, broken up, lay low. Levine probably changed hotels several times before moving to Rue Lepic. For safety, he never appeared with Gloria outside, and they even went so far as to avoid spending the night in the same place.

"Moss must have come to Place d'Anvers every morning to keep in touch. All he had to do was take a seat at the end of the bench.

"Now, as you know, my wife sat down three or four times on that same bench before her dentist appointments. The two women got acquainted and would chat. Moss probably noticed Madame Maigret, but paid no attention to her.

"Imagine his reaction when he found out from the magazine that the good woman on the bench was none other than the wife of the chief inspector in charge of the investigation!

"He couldn't believe it was accidental, could he? He must, quite naturally, have thought that we were on his track and that I had turned over this delicate piece of sleuthing to my wife.

"He rushed over to Rue Lepic and alerted Levine, who dashed out to warn Gloria."

"What was the argument about?"

"Perhaps about the child. Maybe Levine didn't want Gloria to go back for him, and thus run the risk of being arrested. She insisted on going, but with maximum precautions.

"This also inclines me to think that when we find them again, they won't be together. They'll figure that we know Gloria and the boy, whereas we know nothing about Levine. He must have gone off in one direction and Moss in another."

"Do you expect to catch them?"

"Maybe tomorrow, maybe a year from now. You know how things go."

"You still haven't told me where you found the suitcase."

"Perhaps you would prefer not to know how we got possession of it. I was, in fact, forced to use slightly illegal methods, for which I take sole responsibility, but you couldn't possibly approve them.

"All you need to know is that it was Liotard who relieved Steuvels of the compromising suitcase.

"For some reason or other, on that Saturday night Moss took the suitcase to Rue de Turenne and left it there.

"Frans Steuvels simply shoved it under a table in his workshop, thinking no one would bother about it.

"On February 21, Lapointe invented a pretext to be admitted and searched the place.

"Remember that Steuvels couldn't get in touch with his brother or any other member of the gang, probably, to let them know what was going on. I have a theory about that. . . .

"He must have wondered how to get rid of the suitcase, and was doubtless waiting until after dark to see about it, when Liotard, whom he'd never heard of, turned up."

"How did Liotard get to know?"

"Through an indiscretion in my department."

"One of your inspectors?"

"I don't blame him for it, and there's not much chance that it will ever happen again. In any case, Liotard offered his services, even going a bit beyond what one is entitled to expect from a member of the bar, since he disposed of the suitcase."

"Did you find it at his place?"

"At Alfonsi's. He'd passed it on to him."

"Where do we stand now?"

"Nowhere . . . I mean, we know nothing about the essential thing—the two murders. A man was killed on Rue de Turenne, and before that Countess Panetti was killed in her car—where, we don't know. You must have received a report from Dr. Paul, who found a bullet in the old woman's cranium. . . .

"However, a small item of information has reached me from Italy. More than a year ago, the Krynkers were divorced, in Switzerland—since divorce is impossible in Italy. Countess Panetti's daughter regained her liberty to marry an American, with whom she is now living in Texas."

"There was never a reconciliation with her mother?"

"On the contrary. Her mother was more furious with her than ever. Krynker is a Hungarian of good family but poor. He spent part of the winter in Monte Carlo, trying to make his fortune by gambling—with no success.

"He arrived in Paris three weeks before the death of his ex-mother-in-law, and lived at the Commodore, then in a small hotel on Rue Caumartin."

"How long had Gloria Lotti been in the countess's service?"

"Four or five months. That hasn't been determined exactly."

A sound was heard in the corridor, and the old receptionist came to announce that the prisoner had arrived.

"Am I to tell him all this?" asked Dossin, whose responsibilities were weighing on him again.

"There are two possibilities: either he'll talk or he'll keep on refusing to. I've had dealings with several men from Flanders in my time, and I've learned that they're hard to soften up. If he won't talk, it will take weeks—possibly longer. We'll have to wait, in fact, until we rout out one of the four characters holed up Lord knows where."

"Four?"

"Moss, Levine, the woman, and the child, and our best bet may be the child."

"Unless they got rid of him."

"If Gloria went back for him when he was in my wife's charge, she must be attached to him."

"Do you think it's her son?"

"I'm sure of it. It's a mistake to think criminals aren't like other people, that they can't have children and love them."

"Her son by Levine?"

"Probably."

Rising to his feet, Dossin gave a faint smile, which showed a trace of mischief and of humility too.

"This would be the time for a 'grilling,' wouldn't it? Unfortunately, that's not my strong point."

"If you'd allow me, perhaps I could speak to Liotard."

"To get him to advise his client to talk?"

"As matters stand now, it's in their interest—both of them."

"Shall I have them brought in right away?"

"In a moment."

Maigret went out and said cordially to the man sitting to the right of the door, on a bench worn smooth by constant use:

"Good morning, Steuvels."

Just at that moment, Janvier came into the corridor with a very distressed Fernande. The inspector was doubtful about letting her join her husband and deferred to his boss.

"You have time for a chat together," Maigret said to the couple. "The judge isn't quite ready."

He signed to Liotard to follow him, and they talked in undertones as they paced up and down the murky corridor, where there were policemen outside most of the doors. It took barely five minutes.

"When you're ready, knock."

Maigret went into the examining magistrate's room alone, leaving Liotard, Steuvels, and Fernande in conversation.

"Result?" Dossin asked.

"We'll see. Liotard's going along, obviously. I'll cook up a nice little report for you in which I'll mention the suitcase without emphasizing it."

"Isn't that a bit irregular?"

"Do you want to catch the murderers?"

"I understand you, Maigret. But my father and my grandfather were on the bench too, and I want to end my days there."

He was blushing as he waited for the knock on the door with a mixture of impatience and misgiving.

At last it opened.

"Shall I bring Madame Steuvels in too?" asked the lawyer.

Fernande had been crying and held her handkerchief in her hand. She immediately tried to catch Maigret's eye to give him a look of distress, as though she felt confident that he could put everything right.

Steuvels hadn't changed. He was still wearing the expression that was gentle and stubborn at the same time. He went and sat down obediently on the chair he was motioned to.

As the clerk was about to take his place, Dossin said to him:

"Wait. I'll call you when the interrogation becomes official. Are you agreeable, Maître Liotard?"

"Quite, thank you."

Maigret was the only one standing now. He was facing the window, down which little raindrops were rolling. The Seine was gray, like the sky; barges, roofs, sidewalks reflected the wetness.

After two or three little coughs, Judge Dossin's voice was heard, saying diffidently:

"I believe the chief inspector would like to put a few questions to you, Steuvels."

Maigret, who had just lighted his pipe, had no alternative but to turn around, trying to suppress a smile of amusement.

"I suppose," he began, still standing, as if he were addressing a class, "your counsel has briefly given you the picture. We know what you and your brother have been up to. Possibly, as far as you personally are concerned, we have nothing else to charge you with.

"It was not, in fact, your suit that showed traces of blood, but that of your brother, who left his suit with you and took yours away with him."

"My brother didn't commit murder either."

"Probably not. Do you want me to interrogate you, or would you rather tell us what you know?"

Not only was Maître Liotard on the chief inspector's side now, but Fernande, by the look in her eyes, was urging her husband to talk.

"Question me. I'll see if I can answer."

He wiped the thick lenses of his glasses while he waited, round-shouldered, head bent slightly forward, as if it were too heavy.

"When did you learn that Countess Panetti had been killed?"

160

"Saturday night."

"You mean the night Moss, Levine, and a third person, probably Krynker, came to your house?"

"Yes."

"Was it your idea to send a telegram to get your wife out of the way?"

"I wasn't even told about it."

This was plausible. Alfred Moss was sufficiently familiar with the couple's domestic habits and way of life.

"So when someone knocked at your door about nine o'clock that evening, you didn't know what it was about?"

"Yes. Anyhow, I didn't want to let them in. I was reading peacefully in the basement."

"What did your brother tell you?"

"That one of his companions needed a passport that evening, and he'd brought everything along and said I'd better get to work."

"Was that the first time he'd brought strangers to your house?"

"He knew I didn't want to see anyone."

"But you knew he had accomplices?"

"He'd told me he was working with a man named Schwartz."

"The man who called himself Levine at the hotel on Rue Lepic? A rather fat man, very dark?"

"Yes."

"You all went down to the basement together?"

"Yes. I couldn't do anything in the workshop at that time of night or the neighbors would have wondered why."

"Tell me about the third man."

"I didn't know him."

"Did he have a foreign accent?"

"Yes. He was a Hungarian. He seemed anxious to get

away, and he kept asking if he wouldn't run into trouble
with a false passport."

"For what country?"

"The United States. They're the hardest to fake, because of certain special marks known only to consuls and
the Immigration Service."

"So you started work?"

"I didn't have time."

"What happened?"

"Schwartz was inspecting the apartment, as if he was
making sure no one could take us by surprise. Suddenly,
while I had my back turned—I was bending over the
suitcase, which was on a chair—I heard a shot. I turned
and saw the Hungarian slumping to the floor."

"Was it Schwartz who fired?"

"Yes."

"Did your brother seem surprised?"

A moment's hesitation.

"Yes."

"What happened next?"

"Schwartz maintained that this was the only possible
way out, and that it wasn't his fault. According to him,
Krynker had lost his nerve and would surely have been
caught. If he'd been caught, he would have talked.

" 'I was wrong to treat him like a man,' he added.

"Then he asked me where the furnace was."

"He knew there was one?"

"I think so."

Through Moss, obviously; as it was obvious also that
Steuvels did not want to incriminate his brother.

"He ordered Alfred to start a fire and asked me to
bring some very sharp tools.

"Then he said: 'We're all in the same boat, friends. If
I hadn't shot this idiot, we'd have been arrested within

a week. Nobody saw him with us. Nobody knows he's here. He has no family to start making inquiries. Let's get him out of the way, and we'll be all right.' "

This wasn't the moment to ask the bookbinder if they had all helped with the dismemberment.

"Did he tell you about the old woman's death?"

"Yes."

"Was this the first you'd heard of it?"

"I hadn't seen anybody since they left in the car."

He was becoming more reticent, and Fernande's glance was traveling from her husband's face to Maigret's.

"Speak out, Steuvels. They got you into it and then left you holding the bag. What good is it going to do you to keep quiet?"

Maître Liotard added:

"In my capacity as your counsel, I can tell you that it's not only your duty to speak out, but it's in your own interest too. I think the court will take your frankness into consideration."

Steuvels looked at him with big worried eyes and shrugged his shoulders slightly.

"They spent part of the night in my cellar," he finally brought out. "It took a very long time."

A sudden heave of her stomach made Fernande put her handkerchief to her mouth.

"Schwartz—or Levine; never mind his name—had a bottle of brandy in his overcoat pocket, and my brother drank a lot.

"At one point Schwartz said to him, looking furious:

" 'This is the second time you've pulled this one on me.'

"And that was when Alfred told me about the old woman."

"Just a minute," interrupted Maigret. "What, exactly, do you know about Schwartz?"

"He was the man my brother was working for. Alfred talked to me about him several times. He thought he was pretty tough, and dangerous. Schwartz has a child by a pretty girl, an Italian. He lives with her most of the time."

"Gloria Lotti?"

"Yes. . . . Schwartz worked mainly in the big hotels. He'd found a very rich, eccentric woman, and he expected to get a lot out of her. He'd made Gloria take the job as her maid."

"And Krynker?"

"I really only saw him dead, because the shot was fired when he'd only been in my place a few minutes. . . . There are some things I didn't understand until later, when I thought about it."

"For instance?"

"That Schwartz had prepared the whole thing in minute detail. He wanted to get Krynker out of the way, and he'd hit upon this method of doing it without running any risk. When he came that night, he knew what was going to happen. He'd already sent Gloria to Concarneau to send the telegram to Fernande."

"And the old woman?"

"I wasn't mixed up in that business. I know only that, since his divorce, Krynker, who was hard up, had tried to get in touch with her. Recently he'd succeeded, and she sometimes gave him small amounts of money. This immediately melted away, because he liked to live well. . . . What he wanted was enough money to get to the United States."

"Was he still in love with his wife?"

"I don't know. . . . He met Schwartz—or, really,

Schwartz, tipped off by Gloria, managed to meet him in a café—and they became more or less friendly."

"Was it on the night of Krynker's death that they told you all this?"

"We had to wait hours while—"

"Yes, yes."

"I wasn't told whether it was Krynker's idea or whether Schwartz had suggested it to him. Apparently the old woman was in the habit of traveling with a case containing jewelry worth a fortune.

"It was about the time of year when she usually went to the Riviera. It was just a matter of inducing her to go in Krynker's car.

"On the way, at a prearranged point, the car would be put out of commission and the jewel case stolen.

"In Krynker's mind, this was to be managed without bloodshed. He was convinced that he wasn't running any risk, since he would be in the car with his former mother-in-law.

"For some reason, Schwartz fired, and I think he did it on purpose, because this put the other two at his mercy."

"Your brother too?"

"Yes. The attack took place on the Fontainebleau road. Afterward, they drove as far as Lagny to get rid of the car. Schwartz lived in a cottage somewhere near there at one time and was familiar with the district.

"What else do you want to know?"

"Where are the jewels?"

"They found the case, all right, but the jewelry wasn't in it. Probably the countess had her suspicions, after all. Gloria, who was with her, knew nothing about it either. Maybe she left them in a bank."

"That's when Krynker lost his head?"

"He wanted to try to get across the border right away, on his own papers, but Schwartz insisted he'd be caught. He wasn't sleeping at all and was drinking a lot. He was about to panic, so Schwartz decided the only way to get any peace was to get rid of him. . . . He brought him to my place on the pretext of obtaining a false passport for him."

"Why was your brother's suit—"

"At one point, Alfred stumbled, exactly where—"

"So you gave him your blue suit and kept his and cleaned it the next day?"

Fernande's head must have been full of bloody pictures. She was looking at her husband as though seeing him for the first time, no doubt trying to imagine him during the days and nights he had subsequently lived through alone in the basement and the workshop.

Maigret saw her shudder, but the next moment she held out a hesitant hand, which finally came to rest on the bookbinder's big paw.

"Perhaps they have a bindery in prison," she said, making an effort to smile.

Levine, whose name was not Schwartz or Levine, but Sarkistian, was wanted by the authorities of three countries. He was arrested a month later in a little village near Orléans, where he was spending his time fishing.

Two days later, Gloria Lotti was found in a brothel in Orléans. She steadfastly refused to reveal the name of the peasants to whom she had entrusted her son.

As for Alfred Moss, his description remained on the police wanted list for four years.

One night, in a little circus that was traveling from village to village along the roads of the Nord, a down-at-heel clown hanged himself. From an examination of the papers found in his suitcase, the police discovered his identity.

Countess Panetti's jewels had not left the Claridge, having been locked in one of the trunks left in the baggage room.

And the shoemaker on Rue de Turenne never admitted, not even when he was dead drunk, that it was he who had written the anonymous note.